The Hideaway

'He gave a last look ro[...]
happened, he was glad [...] up a
chalky stone and scrap[...] words 'Peter's Den' on
the inside of the rock face. Now it was his. Then he
crawled out into the rain.'

JAMILA GAVIN

The Hideaway

Illustrated by Jane Bottomley

A Magnet Book

Also by Jamila Gavin

Kamla and Kate
The Magic Orange Tree and Other Stories

First published in 1987
by Methuen Children's Books Ltd
This Magnet edition first published in 1988
by Methuen Children's Books
A Division of OPG Services Ltd
Michelin House, 81 Fulham Road, London SW3 6RB
Text copyright © 1988 Jamila Gavin
Illustrations copyright © 1988 Jane Bottomley
Printed in Great Britain by
Cox & Wyman Ltd, Reading

ISBN 0 416 10212 3

Contents

I
The gift

The bike leaned up against the shed. It wasn't new, Peter could see that straightaway, but it looked as if someone had made an effort with it. Though spotted with rust, the handlebars had been rubbed till they gleamed; even the spokes of the wheels had been polished, and managed to glint in the sunlight.

'It's for you,' his mother said in a flat voice.

Peter couldn't believe it. She wasn't like that – giving things out of the blue without a reason. Usually he had to earn everything. He had to come top in his class, or pass his piano exam.

'Oh, Mum!' A surge of love overwhelmed him. Even before he touched the bike, he rushed over to her and flung his arms round her waist.

He felt her body go rigid. 'Don't be soppy now,' she said, pushing him further away. 'I haven't given it you. Your father called round with it.'

'Dad? Is Dad here?' cried Peter.

'No, he's not,' said his mother coldly. 'He's got to make an appointment first, he knows that. He can't just come round whenever he feels like it, the courts made that quite clear.'

Peter felt his excitement turn to anxiety. He went over to the bike and held the handlebars. 'I wish I could have seen him, anyway,' he said quietly.

'Yes . . . well . . .' his mother shrugged. 'You'll see him in a fortnight, as arranged, but I hope he doesn't make a habit of spoiling you. He should have kept the bike for your birthday, but he wouldn't take it back.'

Peter clutched the handles and drew the bike close to him. 'So it is mine?' he said fearfully.

'Yes, it's yours – but don't you go misbehaving, or that bike goes.'

Peter swung himself joyfully on to the saddle. It was almost too high for him. The tips of his toes just touched the ground on each side, and his fingers had to stretch out to their full extent to reach the brakes.

'Can I ride it now?'

'Of course not,' snapped his mother. 'You know you've got your violin lesson in half an hour, and how much homework have you got tonight?'

'Not much,' murmured Peter. But he knew it was no use arguing. No use trying to explain the feelings pounding through him. He lifted the bike against the shed and followed her indoors.

Annabel Colston and her son, Peter, had been living in Randall for just three months now. Annabel kept herself to herself and wouldn't let Peter mix with the village children either. They used to live in London until she and Andy got divorced. It had been a noisy and quarrelsome marriage. Peter could hardly remember a time when his mother and

8

father weren't shouting at each other. Then when Andy began to knock Annabel about, she took Peter and left home. 'We'll have a better life in the country,' she said. So they came to Randall, a small village on the edge of a country town, and moved into a modest stone cottage, with a rambling overgrown garden.

Now they sat at the kitchen table in silence. As usual, tea time was a perfectly organised affair. A plate of thinly sliced brown bread and butter was placed in the middle of the table, while by Peter's plate was a glass of milk, and one chocolate biscuit. His mother poured herself a cup of tea from an elegant china teapot and sipped it slowly, her eyes staring into space all the while.

Outside, Peter could hear the neighbourhood children coming home from school. Their school was only up the lane and each morning they trooped along the road together, chattering and laughing, and each afternoon they returned full of shouts and calls; 'See you after tea!' or 'Let's take the raft on the stream!' or 'Coming biking? I know a good place to go scrambling!'

'Let's go biking!' Peter heard it now. He looked at his mother. 'I wish I could go, I wish I could go,' he pleaded with her silently. But she just stared into space and sipped her tea. She didn't seem to hear the voices in the lane, and she didn't see the look of longing on Peter's face.

Didn't these children ever have homework, or music lessons, or extra French like he did? While he was struggling with French verbs or scales on the violin, they played and played.

'Why can't I go to the school up the lane?' he asked.

'Because you'd never do any work,' answered his mother

9

sharply. 'I don't want you going to the Comprehensive and picking up bad habits. That won't get you anywhere. Of course, if you don't get the scholarship to Allendale, you may have to. I can't pay those sort of school fees on my salary. So don't let me down, Peter. Work hard! Do you hear me?'

Peter heard her. There was no way you couldn't. She had a way of being heard and obeyed. Listlessly, he finished his milk and got his violin and music together. Soon it would be time to get in the car and drive to his violin teacher. They would pass the children milling around in the road, they would pass the stream where the children fished from the banks or played with the rafts, and they would pass the woods – the deep, green, mysterious woods, so full of adventures and secrets and places to hide. One day, he would ride his bike down the lane, on and on until he reached those woods, and then he'd explore, Peter decided this suddenly, as he put his music into the music case. He looked up feeling guilty, wondering if his mother had read his thoughts, but she was clearing away the tea things.

Suddenly there was a knock on the door. Peter and his mother looked at each other, puzzled. They weren't at all used to visitors. She pulled the door open almost fiercely. Two children stood there, a boy about nine, Peter's age, and a girl of about eleven. Peter knew their faces, they were Charlotte and Jack Kimberley who lived at the far end of the village.

'Yes?' His mother asked abruptly.

'Would you like to buy a raffle ticket?' asked Jack.

'We're in a bit of a hurry,' said Annabel Colston rapidly.

'Got to go out. Are you ready, Peter?' She brushed past the children and went to the car.

Peter grabbed his violin case.

'I play the violin,' said Charlotte.

'Do you?' Peter looked surprised and frowned. 'Do you have homework too?' he asked.

'Sometimes,' replied Charlotte cheerfully. 'Why don't you buy a raffle ticket? You could win a bike.'

'I've already got one,' replied Peter.

'I've never seen you on one,' said Jack.

'Well, I have,' cried Peter defiantly. Suddenly he remembered he had 10p in his pocket. 'What other prizes are there?' he asked.

'A car radio,' said Jack.

'OK. I'll buy a ticket,' said Peter, 'and if I win the radio, I'll give it to my dad.'

'Peter!' His mother's voice was shrill and impatient. 'Come on, we're going to be late.' Peter handed over the 10p and grabbed the raffle ticket.

'What's your name?' yelled Jack, as Peter raced to the car.

'Peter! Peter Colston!'

It was eight o'clock before Peter had finally finished with music and homework. He felt dead inside. He knew it was too late to ride the bike. It was still light. Summer had lengthened the evenings, and there were still the voices of children echoing outside.

'Can I have a short ride, please, Mum?' pleaded Peter. 'Please let me just try the bike.'

'If it weren't for that bike, you would have got through your homework quicker,' retorted Annabel Colston. 'Perhaps

11

you'll concentrate better tomorrow. Go to bed now. I can't have you yawning over your desk.'

'I hate you!' The words flew out of his mouth before he realised it. Peter clamped his mouth with his hand in horror.

'Get to bed!' rasped his mother, and he felt the stinging slap burning his cheek as he stumbled from the room.

Peter lay in bed. Tears of anger still poured down his cheeks. His mother passed his door and a shaft of yellow light cut through the darkness as she came in. She stood at the foot of the bed.

'It's for your own good, Peter,' she said. Was this her way of saying she was sorry? He didn't reply. 'You may hate me now,' she continued, 'but one day you'll thank me.' The shaft of light disappeared and she was gone. Peter's rage subsided. He didn't hate her but why did she seem to stand between him and everything he wanted?

The light outside faded. At last, the tantalising noises of the children were gone. Peter wondered what his mother was doing downstairs, all alone. He thought about his bike. Was it still leaning up against the shed? He couldn't sleep, couldn't sleep. He slid out of bed and pushed his bedroom door open. All was quiet. There was only the slow ticking of the grandfather clock, and the hum of the fridge in the kitchen. He stepped out on to the landing. The floorboards creaked. He stopped dead, his heart beating. What was he doing? He hardly thought; he just continued to tiptoe towards the stairs. His mother must have gone to bed. The house was in darkness and there was no slit of light beneath her bedroom door. Slowly and steadily, he walked downstairs and went into the kitchen. The bolt was drawn across the kitchen door. With both hands, he began to ease it up and down, up and down until it slid almost noiselessly across. A turn of the knob, and the door opened and Peter was outside.

The bike was still there, its handlebars gleaming through the darkness, waiting to be ridden. Peter lifted it down the path so that the whirring wheels shouldn't alert his mother. Then, when he had got to the road, he stood there: a funny little figure in his stripy pyjamas and bare feet. Then with a little wobbling, he swung on to the saddle and cycled down the road.

2
A time
to ride

Next morning Andy rang up wanting to speak to Peter. Annabel was annoyed.

'Why do you ring at this time?' she asked coldly. 'You know we're always in a rush getting off to school.' She handed the telephone to Peter. 'Make it quick,' she urged.

'Did you like your bike, Peter?' asked his father.

'Yes, Dad! It's brilliant! Thanks a million!' answered Peter warmly.

'Have you ridden it yet?'

Peter nearly said 'yes', then stopped in confusion. 'Er . . . sort of!' he stammered, glancing warily at Annabel.

'What do you mean, "sort of"?' Andy picked up his hesitation in a flash. 'Your mother's not stopped you riding it, has she?'

Peter could hear his anger boiling up. 'No, Dad! No!' he lied. 'The bike's brilliant, really!'

'Huh!' Andy snorted suspiciously on the other end.

In the brief pause, Peter could hear Radio One blaring out. It reminded him of how there was always music when

Dad was around. Annabel made waving gestures to tell Peter to stop talking.

'I'd better go now, Dad. We'll be late.'

'See you a week Saturday,' said Andy. 'OK, pardner?'

'OK, pardner!' replied Peter with a grin. He and his dad always rounded off an agreement with those words then spat in the palms of their right hands and shook on it.

Annabel plonked a bowl of porridge on the table. 'Come on! Eat up!' she said. 'I suppose he wanted to know if you'd tried the bike.'

'Sort of,' murmured Peter. He felt a sudden lump rise in his stomach. He didn't feel hungry, but he knew he wouldn't be allowed to leave the table until he'd eaten it all up. Slowly, he carved channels out of the porridge with the side of his spoon. The milk ran into them and broke the porridge up into islands. He wondered if his mother would guess that he had sneaked out in the night like a thief and ridden the bike.

'Oh do stop playing with your food,' pleaded Annabel.

Peter began to swallow the porridge, island by sugary island, while his mother checked his school timetable.

'Maths . . . English . . . History . . . I hope you get an A for that last History homework. I expect you'll find out today.'

Peter nodded dully. A was the only mark that counted with Annabel, and he hardly ever got one. If only he could put bike riding down on the timetable too. There must be a way. Peter began trying to work it out in his mind.

They set off for school, opening the door of Trimble cottage at exactly the same time as they did every morning. They passed the local school children straggling along the lane to their village school. He knew them all by sight, even if he didn't play with them. When he had been allowed out, he would hang round the lanes like a stray dog, just watching. Sometimes he followed them, but always at a distance, never getting close. He knew who was friends with whom, and who enemies. But if anyone said, 'Do you want to play?' he would back off shyly and say, 'I'm not allowed.'

Now, as they swept past them in the car on the way to Allendale, he ducked down as he did every morning. Once when they'd seen him in his grey and maroon school uniform they'd called out, 'Poshy! Toshy! Snob, snob, snob!' But he only wished he was one of them.

This particular morning he noticed Charlotte Kimberley was carrying her violin. 'When does she get time to practise and still play outside each afternoon,' he wondered. He thought about it all day and got told off for daydreaming. Then suddenly he had an idea. If he got up a bit earlier and practised the violin before breakfast, he would have at least half an hour more each afternoon. He would start tomorrow.

Granny Colston had once told Peter that if you want to wake at, say, seven o'clock in the morning, you must bang your head seven times on the pillow before going to sleep at night. The first time he tried it, he failed and awoke far too early in pitch darkness. The second time he didn't wake at all until Annabel came in as usual at seven-thirty. At last, after another failed attempt, he awoke one morning at exactly seven o'clock.

Triumphantly, he dressed, tiptoed downstairs and began to practise his violin.

'What the dickens are you doing?' His mother appeared in the doorway, all ruffled with sleep.

'I just woke up early,' explained Peter, carefully not mentioning the bike. 'I thought I'd practise before breakfast. My teacher thinks mornings are a good time.' This was true, although when his teacher had suggested it, Peter had thought it was a terrible idea.

Annabel frowned and muttered something. Peter wondered if she would stop him. Instead she went into the kitchen, put on the kettle and lit a cigarette. She had started smoking since they moved to the country, and Peter wished she wouldn't.

'Granny says smoking gives you cancer,' he warned. Annabel didn't answer, so Peter went on practising.

'I suppose this early morning practising lark will be a nine-day wonder,' she remarked finally. 'But if you must do it, go into the dining-room in future where you won't wake me.'

It was drizzling as they drove up the lane. Peter prayed that the weather would clear so that he could go bike riding after school. All through the day as he rushed from one classroom to another the thought of his bike shone like a beacon. Even when he was told he had only got B minus for History, he didn't care. He watched the hands of the clock moving slowly but steadily round until the final bell went.

Annabel worked at an antique shop in the nearby town, Dudridge. She dropped Peter off at school and then collected him again at four o'clock. Usually he dawdled out, and spent a bit of time messing around. Today he came charging out and flung himself into her little red mini with an exuberance she found surprising.

'Did you get A for History?' she asked.

'No, we haven't heard yet,' lied Peter. 'I'm so glad it's stopped raining.' He was thrilled to see the sunshine sparkling in the wet bushes, and pulled off his school cap as a first stage to getting out of his uniform.

'You should have heard by now,' frowned his mother.

> 'Crisscross the Bible, never tell a lie,
> For if you do your mother will die.'

Peter felt a lump growing in his stomach again. There would be trouble if Annabel found out but he thought, 'If there's going to be trouble, let it be after I've ridden my bike.'

As soon as they got home, Peter completed the change from uniform into jeans and tee shirt, and got down to his homework. Already he could hear the children in the lane. He struggled to concentrate. His mother always looked over his homework and made him do it again if it wasn't correct or tidy enough.

At last it was done, just as Annabel put tea on the table. He tried not to wolf down his bread and butter and gulp his milk, and he tried not to sound too eager when he said, 'I've done all my homework, Mum, and I did my violin this morning. Can I go out and ride my bike?'

Annabel looked faintly surprised as if she had forgotten he had a bike. 'Are you sure you've done everything? You'd better not start getting slapdash just because of some bike. I knew there must be something behind this early morning practice business.' She scrutinized his books. Peter crossed the fingers of both hands. 'She can't find anything wrong, she just can't.'

At last she said, grudgingly, 'Well, I suppose it's all right. You can cycle for half an hour, but don't go into anyone's house, do you understand? And no accepting things from anyone. Nothing.'

Peter nodded energetically and made for the door in case she changed her mind. At last! He lovingly took the handlebars of his bike, and pushed it down the path into the road for the second time.

The late afternoon sun pierced through the sky which was still heavy with grey clouds. It caught the children in a spotlight and outlined them as they wheeled round on their bikes like strange birds. Suddenly, Peter was overcome with shyness. He leaned into the wet grassy bank hoping not to be seen for a while.

He watched them: Jack and Charlotte Kimberley, Sean and Gary, who were twins but who didn't look at all alike, Janet and Michelle, who were hardly ever apart because they were best friends. Then there was Denis Corrie.

Denis Corrie had power. You could see that by the way he rode round on his racer, fast and risky. The children gave into him because they were afraid of him – all except Charlotte. She wasn't afraid of anyone. You wouldn't think it to look at her. She wasn't very big for eleven: rather thin, rather pale, with straight black hair cut in a bob, and no-nonsense blue eyes. But it was her voice that made your toes curl. It was surprising coming out of such a little body, hoarse and commanding. Annabel would have said it was like a fishwife's, but Peter thought she was wonderful. He'd often heard her put Denis in his place.

Suddenly the children stopped what they were doing and looked at him. They seemed to be waiting for him.

Peter didn't move. He still half-leaned into the bank gripping his handlebars. He knew they were expecting him to ride his bike; go through his paces; show them what he could do. He thought they would stay frozen for ever, just staring at each other, when suddenly Jack Kimberley, cocky as a cowboy, cried, 'Watch me!' He cycled off a little way down the lane at top speed. Then he did a racing turn with a squeal of brakes and a shower of gravel, and hurtled back, aiming for a piece of wood that had been placed in the road. He struck, and Jack and his bike sailed through the air. It was pure flight. He bounced back on to the road and didn't stop until he was level with Peter.

'So this is your bike, is it?' said Jack, chucking his own to the ground. 'Where did you get it?'

'My dad gave it to me.' replied Peter.

'Where's your dad, then?' enquired Jack, swinging astride Peter's bike without asking.

'In London,' said Peter, anxious that Jack shouldn't treat his bike as roughly as his own.

'Oh, so he doesn't live with you,' commented Jack.

Peter didn't answer, but picked up Jack's bike. He was about to swap it back for his own, when Denis Corrie rode up like a demon and butted Peter's bike so that Jack wobbled and had to get off.

'Call this a bike!' sneered Denis. 'It's a load of junk!' and he butted it again. Denis leaned his bike against the wall and then came over to examine Peter's. Peter tried to wheel it away, but Denis suddenly wrenched the bike from him, and rode off.

'Hey! Give me back my bike!' Anger and alarm made Peter's voice sound high and trembly.

'Does Poshy Toshy want his bikey back?' mimicked Denis cruelly. 'Then Poshy Snob better come and get it!' He pedalled slowly and carelessly down the road.

Charlotte intervened. She leapt in front of Denis. 'Give it back! You big bully!' She grabbed the handlebars and shook them violently. He tried to kick her out of the way. She jumped aside and began tussling with him from behind. 'Get off, Denis, you great ape!' Then the others all pitched in, grabbing at the bike and yelling at Denis. Peter stood watching in horror, certain his bike would be torn to pieces.

'Denis!' They were interrupted by a raucous voice, which brought them all to a standstill. A large pink-faced woman stood at a cottage gate a little way down the lane. She was wiping her hands on a dish cloth. 'Come on in and have your tea.'

'All right, all right!' Nonchalantly, he dismounted. He paused for a moment, just steadying the bike with his finger tips. 'I was only trying it out, the toffee-nosed little squirt,' he hissed, and took his hands off the bike, letting it crash to the ground.

As Denis walked past the large pink-faced woman, she swiped him round the head with her dishcloth. 'You been messing those kids around, have you?' she demanded, and they disappeared inside, jostling and arguing with each other.

Charlotte picked up Peter's bike and handed it back to him. He hoped she didn't notice how close to tears he was. He quickly bent down and pretended to examine the pedals through blurred eyes.

'Thanks for getting it back,' he murmured.

Suddenly everyone was bored. Charlotte and Michelle said they wanted to go and see Janet's new kittens.

'Do you want one?' Janet asked Peter. 'You can have it free – two if you like – me dad'll drown them if they're not got rid of.'

'I wouldn't be allowed,' said Peter, getting up. He had blinked away his tears and could look them all in the face.

'Let's go scrambling in Badham's Yard!' cried Gary.

'Yeh!' agreed Sean and Jack, leaping on to their bikes. 'You coming too?' they asked Peter.

'I'd better not,' he said.

'See you then!' they cried as they rode off yelling and shouting.

Peter stood, watching till they were out of sight. He looked up and down, but now the lane was empty and he was alone. He saw the piece of wood in the middle of the road. It seemed to challenge him. He got astride his bike and fiercely thrust his foot down on the pedal. He cycled several yards down the lane, then turned – not quite the racing turn Jack had performed – and lined himself up before the lump of wood. He rode furiously towards it, faster, faster, faster. He pedalled, then stopped as his front wheel struck the obstacle with a thud that made him leave the saddle. He felt the bike rise under him. It left the ground, only for a millionth of a second, but it was enough. As Peter bounced back on to the road, a great big grin broke across his face from ear to ear.

'I wish Jack had seen that!'

He went and did it again and again until it was time to go in.

3
Discovery

The lane which ran past Trimble Cottage carried on through the centre of the village like a long grey ribbon. It looped round the little green with the red telephone box on it, past the post office and the dairy; on past the little farm cottages, and Dr Blakely's converted barn house, until it finally broke free of the village and all human habitation and cut out across the lush green meadows where brown and white cows grazed as if they had been there since the world began.

At the far end of the meadow, the long dark skirts of Juggins Wood swept down as if they would engulf everything in their steep plunge, but instead were held back within the smooth contours of the land as if by an invisible force. Here a stream tumbled out of the woods with a fierce rush. As it struck the open flat pastures, it broke up into a myriad of little water courses which ran like silver fingers through the long grass, trapping the bold yellow marsh marigolds, and the tall spiky water irises between their meanderings.

Every day Peter and Annabel drove along this lane to

24

school and work, and every day Peter's yearning to explore Juggins wood grew and grew.

Peter kept up his new routine. Every night he banged his head seven times on the pillow before going to sleep, and every morning he awoke at seven to do his violin practice. Mostly it worked and he got in a quick ride, but he was looking forward to Saturday afternoon when he would have a longer time to ride – perhaps long enough to ride to Juggins Wood. He asked Jack about it.

'I might be free Saturday morning,' Jack said.

'I've got school on Saturday morning,' replied Peter mournfully.

Jack looked at him with a mixture of horror and pity when he heard that, and said, 'I'll try and play in the afternoon, but we may have something on.'

He did have something on. Peter didn't find out till Saturday afternoon when he pushed his bike out into the lane and looked up and down wondering where everyone was.

'They're all up at the school,' said a low hoarse voice. 'It's their fête.'

Peter turned, startled, and then saw the old man sitting half-hidden on a low stone wall. Peter knew his name was Percy Crimpwell. Old Percy was the eyes and ears and tongue of the village. He often walked ten or fifteen miles a day pushing an old black pram in which he collected bits of firewood, pausing every now and then to sit on a wall, lean over a gate or beg a cup of tea at a friendly kitchen door.

'I bought a raffle ticket.' Percy thrust a thin knuckly hand into the depths of his old, overlarge, brown winter coat, and pulled out a crumpled ticket. 'First prize is a bicycle.' He eyed Peter's bike. 'You won't be needing one of those, I don't suppose. Wouldn't be much use to me neither.' He sniffed and rubbed his nose vigorously along his sleeve.

'Perhaps you'll win the car radio,' said Peter. 'That's what I want.'

'Not much use to me, a car radio, seeing as how I ain't got no vehicle,' cackled Percy. 'But I tell you which prize I'd really like.' He leaned forward confidentially, resting on the pram's handlebars. 'I would like old Doris Sidley's carrot cake. She bakes a beautiful cake does old mother Sidley, I can tell you, and she always bakes one for the raffle. Does your mother bake a good cake?' The old man's eyes, red-rimmed and watery as they were, suddenly looked sharply at Peter.

'Sometimes,' answered Peter, suddenly unable to meet his gaze. Then he said, 'I bought a raffle ticket too. I hope someone will tell me if I win.'

'Oh yes,' nodded the old man. 'You needn't worry about that – but you should be up there. They always put on a good show.'

'I think I'll just ride my bike. Bye, Percy!' and Peter swung astride his bike and pedalled off down the road.

When Peter reached the end of the village, he paused and looked at the water meadows stretching before him and, at the far end, Juggins Wood, a dark mysterious blob between land and sky. He felt as if he stood at the frontier of a new country, and he wished Jack was with him to be his guide. His eye followed the grey lane as it now ran in a dead straight line until it disappeared into the trees.

Peter began to pedal faster. Faster and faster he rode, till his leg muscles burned and the wind rushed into his face. Within seconds he had crossed the water meadows and left behind the open land dotted with cows. Abruptly, the lane forged into the woods and the trees arched round him like a tunnel. Peter found himself flying along between high steep banks. Beyond the banks, layer upon layer of trees climbed thickly up the hillside, full of hanging creepers and dark hollows; full of twitterings and rustlings, and the scurrying of unseen animals. They seemed to be waiting for him; listening and watching.

Without warning, he came to a break in the bank and saw a narrow track leading into the very depths of the wood. He swung off the smooth metalled road and bounced on to the raw ground. He got off his bike and stood for a moment, bewildered, like a stranger entering a new land. Then as he looked at the track rising up, tantalising; beckoning; he felt the primitive excitement of discovery and the feeling of ownership – finders keepers! He didn't consider for a moment that others had been to these woods before him. For the moment, they were his and, if he'd had a flag, he would have planted it.

Peter looked around for somewhere to hide his bike. He lifted it carefully over the undergrowth so that it wouldn't get scratched and lowered it gently into the long grass in a spot well camouflaged by blackthorn bushes. Back on the path once more, he couldn't even see the bike himself, so he started along the grassy track, following it up and up. Somewhere ahead he could hear the stream rushing and gurgling. He decided to find it.

The path drew him on and on, climbing and climbing till he was panting hard and his legs felt weak. Suddenly, the ground levelled out, and the path veered sharply to the left and plunged into wild holly trees. Prickly branches bent over in long tangles and clutched at his sweater. He paused, breathing hard, trying to hear the stream above the rapid thudding of his heart.

Peter left the track and began following the sound of the stream somewhere to the right.

It wasn't so easy. The ground was tangled with briars, and roots of trees sprawled out unexpectedly to trip him up. But he struggled on until suddenly he emerged into a small grassy clearing – and there it was!

The stream came bouncing noisily out of the rocky undergrowth. It swirled round a large boulder and then ran flat for a few metres, broadening out into a natural pool. Here it seemed to rest for a while, calm and reflective, before gathering itself together again, rushing out as a waterfall on the other side, and pitching itself down the steep stony gully.

Peter ran forward with delight. It was like a playground. There were trees with long hairy creepers to swing on; rocks and stones and fallen branches to heave into the pool to make channels, harbours and dams.

Bursting with energy, he tore off his shoes and socks, rolled up his trousers and waded into the water. For a while he ran in and out and round in all directions trying out everything, then he concentrated on heaving the stones over to the shallows to make a crossing of stepping stones. He worked so intently that he didn't notice the black clouds rolling across the tops of the trees.

The first drops of rain fell fat and heavy, scarring the smooth surface of the pool with little craters. Peter looked up and groaned. The rain was now falling steadily; already it was penetrating his sweater and shirt, and trickling down the back of his neck. He raced back to his shoes and socks, wondering where to shelter. Most of the trees were tall and slender, their branches too high to give any cover.

Then Peter noticed a thick shield of hawthorn bushes round the base of a steep bit of hillside, where the stream poured out. Perhaps he would find some shelter there. He scrambled towards them, and squeezed himself between the prickly branches. Dropping on to his hands and knees, he crawled towards the rock face.

'Fantastic!' Peter cried out loud. He found himself staring into the opening of a small dry cave. He curled himself inside and put on his shoes and socks.

There seemed to be no let up in the rain. Peter looked at his watch. He'd been out nearly an hour. He began to feel nervous. He ought to get home – not that Annabel had given him a time, but then she thought he was just outside in the lane. If he tried to go home now he'd get soaked through and his mum would be furious. If he waited for the rain to stop he'd be late back and she'd still be furious. The lump came back to his stomach. All the excitement of the stream disappeared; he stared miserably out at the pouring rain.

He hugged his knees to his chest and looked round his little shelter. At least it was dry and protected. He liked the smell of the earth and dry leaves, and the solid feel of the hard rock. Then he noticed that he was crouched in just a niche of the cave which ran deeper into the hillside. He crept a little way down. For a while, the daylight lit his way, but suddenly the ground dipped steeply, and he stared into pitch darkness. He crawled backwards to the opening, back to his niche.

'Next time, I'll bring my torch,' he said, talking to himself. 'Perhaps I'll bring Jack. Perhaps not.' Peter wasn't sure. This cave was a secret. He wanted it to be his cave. His own hideaway.

He peered out through the prickly screen of hawthorn. The rain wasn't going to stop yet, and he couldn't stay here forever. He would have to make a dash for home.

He gave a last look round the cave. Whatever happened, he was glad he had found it. He picked up a chalky stone and scraped the words 'Peter's Den' on the inside of the rock face. Now it was his. Then he crawled out into the rain.

It wasn't easy finding his way back, what with the rain and the slippery wetness. He wasn't sure where he had left the path. He stumbled and fell down the dripping hillside, sliding and slithering from one tree trunk to another. Peter could only hope that by going downwards he would eventually hit the lane.

He did, but much further round from the spot where he had entered the woods. The rain blinded him as he ran, searching desperately for the track. The road rounded a bend and he almost rushed past it. Just in time, he recognized one of the tall trees. He plunged into the shrubbery to hunt for his bike.

'Dear God, please let me find it. Dear God, please let it not be lost!' he prayed. He must have circled the bicycle several times in his panic before he almost fell over it. Half-choked with relief, he hauled it out on to the road, and set off for home.

He tried to ride fast but his legs wouldn't go round. It was as if the road had turned to syrup, clogging the bicycle wheels so that it took all his effort to pedal just one turn of the wheel. At last the first cottages came into sight. Just then a shabby blue and white van hurtled towards him, its windscreen wipers whisking to and fro and its wheels throwing up spray. Peter wondered if it had seen him, for it didn't slow down, and he was forced to lean into the bank, half falling off his bike.

As it flashed by, Peter just caught a glimpse of Denis Corrie, sitting up front next to his dad. In that brief moment they both turned and stared at him. Denis pulled a face, evil and sneering, and then they were gone. Peter felt uneasy. He knew now that Denis was his enemy.

He cycled the last stretch to his door slowly, almost reluctantly. Time made no difference now. He would be in trouble whatever he did. Wearily he hauled his bike up the path and put it in the shed then with a small sigh, he opened the kitchen door and went in.

'My goodness! You look as though you've been up the Amazon!' exclaimed a cheery voice.

Peter stood in the doorway, bedraggled and amazed. It was Jack's mother, Mrs Kimberley, sitting there at the kitchen table drinking a cup of tea.

Annabel stood up, her eyes furious. 'Where have you been?' she asked through clenched teeth.

'Your mother was getting worried about you,' Mrs Kimberley intervened, as if trying to calm the situation. 'I told her you'd probably been scrambling with the boys. You're as bad as my Jack,' she rattled on with a friendly grin. 'The way he goes through his clothes . . .' she glanced warily at Annabel.

'Peter, this is Mrs Kimberley,' she said icily. 'Don't just stand there gawking. Remember your manners.'

Peter held out a wet hand. 'How do you do, Mrs Kimberley,' he murmured.

'I'm very glad to meet you, Peter,' Mrs Kimberley took his hand and squeezed it warmly. 'I've heard all about you from Jack. I can see why you get on, you're a couple of ragamuffins. Mind you, Jack could learn some of your manners.'

'Take off those filthy shoes and get upstairs. You'd better get out of those wet clothes immediately and run a bath,' ordered Annabel, ignoring Mrs Kimberley's friendliness.

'Here! Before you go!' interrupted Mrs Kimberley. 'You won something at the school raffle, Peter. That's why I called in.' She reached into her shopping basket and lifted out a large round cake tin. 'You've won Mrs Sidley's carrot cake! You lucky boy! Course, not all boys like carrot cake, but I'm sure your mother will appreciate it.' She placed it in the centre of the table with a flourish. 'Now I'd best be going.'

As she reached the door and opened it, she turned and watched Peter for a moment as he tugged off his soggy shoes and socks. 'Boys will be boys, won't they, Mrs Colston?' she remarked protectively.

'Yes,' retorted Annabel. 'Give them an inch and they take a yard. Good night, Mrs Kimberley.'

The door shut firmly behind her, and for a few seconds Mrs Kimberley paused. She heard Annabel's shriek of rage inside the cottage. She half turned back, then shrugged her shoulders.

'It's none of my business, I suppose,' she muttered, 'but I reckon that poor lad's in for a hammering.' With a heavy heart, she set off home.

4
Swearing
friendship

Funny how things can go wrong just when you think they are going right. Just when he had fitted bike-riding into his timetable, just when he had started to become quite friendly with the village children – especially Jack, just when he was beginning to feel free, suddenly it all crumbled away on one afternoon.

If only it hadn't rained. If only he hadn't got lost. If only he had got an A for History instead of B minus, Annabel might not have been so angry. Now his bike was locked in the shed and he didn't know when he would be able to ride it again.

Granny Colston used to say, 'It's all water under the bridge,' when she meant that something was over and done with. But it was hard to know with Annabel. Each day since his ride to Juggins Wood Peter had studied his mother's face to see if it were the right moment to find out if it was 'all water under the bridge', but she had gone into one of her silent moods. It was as though she were sleepwalking and the days slid by on automatic control.

Now it was Thursday, five whole days since he had ridden his bike. Annabel had told him to play in the garden where she could see him. Peter had wandered down to the very far end where the grass was high and the bushes overgrown. Here, he felt hidden, secretive. If his mother wanted him, she called.

A thick beech hedge separated the garden of Trimble Cottage from the road. Peter found a small twiggy gap which he could wriggle through on his tummy and peer out into the lane. He could hear the children, Jack, Charlotte, the twins and Janet and Michelle. He would have called out to them, but Denis was there too, circling them like a troublesome wasp, interfering with their games, teasing and quarreling. At last they all started moving further and further down the lane, still in a tight cluster. Only Jack was dawdling behind. Peter was sure he was too far away to hear, but he called out in a piercing whisper, 'Hey, Jack!'

Jack heard. He looked up, at first not seeing him, then when he did, his face broke out into a beaming smile and he cycled over to the hedge.

'Are you coming out on your bike?' he asked cheerily. 'I've got a new trick!'

'I'm not allowed,' said Peter wryly. 'I went to Juggins Wood and got lost.'

'I know,' replied Jack. 'My mum told me.' He began to bounce his bike up and down. 'Look! I've been practising this for ages. I can get both wheels off the ground now.'

Peter watched in silence. At last Jack stopped bouncing and leaned his bike against the bank.

'Did you eat the carrot cake?' he asked.

'Of course not! I hate carrots,' exclaimed Peter pulling a face.

'Me too in stews and things,' agreed Jack, 'but carrot cake is different. It's brilliant!'

'I'll go and get you some, then,' cried Peter. 'Wait there!' He ran back up the garden and into the kitchen. Annabel wasn't there. He could hear the television on in the living-room, so he quietly opened the pantry door and lifted out the cake tin.

When he got back to the bottom of the garden, it was to find Jack leaning up against the old apple tree smiling wickedly. Peter couldn't help looking back to the cottage with alarm, but Jack said, 'Don't worry. I know how to get in and out of this garden like greased lightning. We were always scrumping those apples when old Mrs Critchley lived here.'

The two boys flopped down into the long grass and were quite hidden from the watchful eyes of the cottage windows. Peter levered open the lid of the cake tin. A rich sweet smell rose up into his face, and he sniffed in surprise.

'It smells good,' he murmured.

'Quick, where's a knife?' said Jack, eager to sink his teeth into the cake.

'I forgot about that,' groaned Peter. 'Here, use this.' He fished around in his pocket and produced a penknife.

'Great!' sighed Jack snatching it from him, and lopping off a chunk without much regard to shape or size. 'Try some,' he urged through bulging cheeks, digging in for another piece.

Peter sliced off a tiny corner and tentatively put it on the

36

tip of his tongue. His mouth was filled with a sweet sugary flavour – not in the least like boiled carrots. 'Mmmm,' he admitted slowly. 'It's not too bad,' and he sliced off another piece.

'You know, I've always thought you could build a really good den in this apple tree,' remarked Jack, looking up into the twisted old branches. 'Look, you could put some planks of wood across those two branches there.' He pointed up to where the trunk forked into a Y shape. 'I've got a smashing den in my garden. Course, my dad built it really.'

Peter thought of the cave in Juggins Wood. He meant to keep it his secret, but what use was a secret with no one to share it?

'I've got a den too,' said Peter. 'It's absolutely brilliant.'

'Where?' asked Jack looking around keenly.

'It's not here . . . it's . . .' Peter hesitated. If he told Jack, then Jack might tell Charlotte, and she would tell the girls, and then everyone would know.

'It's . . . it's supposed to be a secret,' muttered Peter. 'I wasn't going to tell.'

Jack looked peeved. He put the lid back on the cake tin. 'Oh well, in that case I'd better be going.' He began to crawl towards the gap in the hedge.

Suddenly they heard Denis's voice. 'Oi! Jack! Where are you?'

Peter and Jack looked at each other. Peter put a finger to his lips, pleading with Jack not to give them away. Jack fell flat on his tummy and wriggled back to the apple tree.

'Where are you. I know you're around. Your bike's here,' hollered Denis. 'Have you gone to visit Poshy Snob and his mother, Mrs Poshy Snob?'

Peter heard the kitchen door fly open, and Annabel rushed down to the gate. 'Go away! Go on! Scram! I won't have rude common boys making a nuisance of themselves round my house. Go away, or I'll have words with your father.'

They heard Denis call back sarcastically, 'All right, all right, Mrs. I'm going,' his voice getting fainter as he cycled away.

'Peter!' Annabel's voice cut across the garden. 'Where are you.'

Signalling to Jack to stay hidden, Peter stood up and shouted, 'I'm here, Mum! I'm just trying to build a den in the apple tree.' He walked up the garden a bit till she could see him.

He thought she would order him in immediately, but she said, 'Stay out of my way for another five minutes. My boss, Mrs Brideworthy, is calling round in half an hour and I need to sort out some drinks and eats.'

Peter went back to Jack who was now sitting with his back up against the tree. He felt in a turmoil. He wanted to tell Jack about the secret cave in Juggins Wood.

'I'd like to show you my den,' said Peter, 'but it's a secret, see?'

'I can keep a secret,' retorted Jack huffily, 'but if you don't want to tell, what do I care.'

He looked as if he were going to go again. Peter stared at him desperately. He liked Jack very much. He liked his round open face and his head of tight, brown, fuzzy hair.

He liked the way he screwed up his eyes when he laughed, and he laughed a lot. He knew he was a show-off, but he was generous. Even if he only had two sweets left, he would offer Peter one of them. Peter had never had a chance to show him any friendship in return. He wasn't allowed sweets and there seemed to be nothing he could give him or share with him. But now he had a chance.

'Will you be best friends?' he asked him.

To Peter's relief, Jack's face broke into a big grin. 'Yeah! Let's be best friends! I've got lots of friends, but I haven't got a best, best friend.' He held out the little finger of his right hand. Peter linked it with the little finger of his right hand and they both shook. They chanted as they shook:

'Make friends, make friends,
Never, never break friends.'

'Now we are friends,' announced Peter, 'and we'll share everything and tell each other everything.'

'If we have secrets,' added Jack, 'we'll never tell anyone else unless we both agree.'

'Cross your heart, cut your throat and hope to die?' asked Peter.

Jack flung his arms across his chest to cross his heart. He licked two fingers and flicked them across his throat and repeated, 'Cross my heart, cut my throat and hope to die.'

'Now shake on it,' ordered Peter. They clasped each other's hands and shook on it.

'Peter!' Annabel's voice broke into the solemnity of their ceremony. 'I want you to come in now, quickly!'

'I'd better go,' Peter gasped, letting go Jack's hand.

39

'You haven't told me the secret yet,' protested Jack.

'It's a cave. A cave in Juggins Wood. I found it by accident. It's so hidden I'd never be able to tell you where it is. I'll have to show you,' whispered Peter all in a rush.

'When?' demanded Jack.

'As soon as I can. As soon as I'm allowed out,' Peter reassured him. 'I must go. Don't let my mum see you here. It would ruin everything.'

'OK.' Jack smiled. It was a warm smile of true friendship. 'I'll sneak off when you've gone. Don't worry. If you're not allowed out, I can always come and meet you here, OK?'

'OK.' The lump in Peter's stomach which had weighed so heavily inside him for days, seemed suddenly to melt away, and there was a small, but joyful smile on his face as he raced back across the garden.

5
Beyond
the mirror

Mrs Brideworthy had just arrived when Peter came in from the garden.

'Wash your hands, Peter,' said Annabel, 'then you can join us in the living-room.'

Peter obeyed, though he would have rather gone upstairs to his room. With a dutiful sigh he turned the door knob slowly. Annabel was sitting in an armchair with a leggy side table drawn up to her right hand. On the table were three or four little plates with things to eat like pastry shells stuffed with mushroom filling, salad dip complete with carrot, celery and cucumber fingers, cheese biscuits already topped with blobs of fish paste or liver pâté.

Mrs Brideworthy sat on the settee with a glass of sherry dangling from her finger tips. She needed the settee because she was an ample, bosomy lady, who spread herself extravagantly in her billowy Indian skirt and black tasselled shawl.

As Peter entered the room Annabel smiled at him. It was the first smile she had given him in days.

'Peter, I'd like you to meet Mrs Brideworthy of Brideworthy Antiques where I work.'

Veiled behind Annabel's smile Peter got her silent message. 'Come on, Peter. Don't let me down. Show Mrs Brideworthy what a well-behaved boy you are.'

Peter held out his hand to Mrs Brideworthy. 'How do you do?'

'What a lovely boy,' gushed Mrs Brideworthy. 'It's so rare to find a boy with manners these days. How do you do, Peter? I'm very glad to meet you.'

When her long red-nailed hand stretched out to grasp his, Peter almost flinched. He had a sudden image of her arm turning into a tentacle and entwining him in her folds. But he was surprised. She squeezed his hand warmly and let it go quickly. She looked him in the eye and cocked her head at him in a friendly sort of way.

Then she and Annabel began to talk business. Peter felt himself becoming invisible, except when Annabel shot him a glance every now and then to hand round the eats.

After a while, a coffee-pot on the side began to bubble noisily. As Annabel went to attend to it she said, 'Peter dear, fetch the carrot cake. It's in the larder. I'm sure Mrs Brideworthy would like some.'

Peter went ashen. He didn't move. The carrot cake was in the garden. He felt turned to stone.

'Peter!' she repeated his name more sharply. 'Did you hear what I said. Fetch the carrot cake.'

'I haven't eaten carrot cake for years,' exclaimed Mrs Brideworthy encouragingly. 'I would love some, please.'

Somehow Peter left the room, closing the door behind him. He fled down the garden to the apple tree. The tin was still lying there in the long grass. Its lid was not quite on, and a trail of little ants crawled up the side and disappeared into its depths.

'Get off! Get off!' Peter almost sobbed as he flicked them away. Cramming the lid back on, he dashed back to the kitchen. He found his mother's best rose-bordered platter on which she always liked to serve cake when she had visitors.

He tipped the carrot cake out on to the platter and groaned with horror. It looked like a crumbled ruin where he and Jack had hacked bits out with the penknife. He tried to press the remains together and reshape it into something resembling a whole cake.

'Peter!' Annabel's voice was puzzled and impatient. 'What are you doing? Bring the cake.'

Swallowing hard, Peter took up the platter and went back to the living-room.

'It was baked by a local woman, Mrs Sidley, who is very well known for her cakes,' Annabel was saying. She swooped up to him and took the platter.

Peter heard his mother's sharp intake of breath. He instinctively braced himself for a blow across the head. It didn't come. Of course. She wouldn't hit him in front of visitors.

'Oh dear!' tittered Mrs Brideworthy. 'It looks as though a bomb has fallen on it.'

'What have you done to it?' demanded Annabel with supressed fury.

'I ate some,' said Peter. 'It's mine, so I thought I could.'

'You thought, you thought . . .' Her rage spilled over in a low outburst. 'Take it away and bring in the sponge cake.'

'Oh, please, do let him cut me a tiny sliver from the good side of the cake. It would be such a pity not to have a little taste – and after all – who cares what it looks like? It is the taste that counts.' Mrs Brideworthy flashed her eyes and used her hands dramatically as if she were miming everything she said. She cocked her head on one side again, and looked coyly at Peter. Peter glanced at Annabel. Annabel plonked the platter down on the side table and turned towards Mrs Brideworthy with an apologetic smile.

'Children always let you down,' she remarked. Then she indicated the knife to Peter. 'Try and cut Mrs Brideworthy a clean, decent slice. Do something right for once, please.'

Carefully, Peter sliced the most solid side of the cake he could find. To his relief, it held together. He managed to slide the flat of the knife underneath the slice and transfer it from the platter to a little side plate.

As Peter handed the plate to Mrs Brideworthy, she extolled him extravagantly. 'That was perfectly executed, Peter. Thank you.' She turned to Annabel. 'I must say, you've done a wonderful job with him. It must be so hard bringing up a boy all on your own.' Peter hoped she wouldn't notice the little ant which crawled along the edge of the plate and disappeared underneath.

Annabel smiled gratefully, as if pleased that someone understood her plight. 'You'd better go and do some homework, Peter,' she said in a 'don't argue' voice. Peter knew that Annabel knew he had already done his homework, but it was a suitable way of getting him to leave the room.

He was glad to leave. He managed to return the wide dazzling smile thrown him by Mrs Brideworthy and went up to his room.

Granny Colston's stream of troubles might float away under her bridge, but Peter's seemed caught up in a dark and ever deepening pool. He sat blankly on the edge of his bed. Opposite him on the wall was an oval mirror. A face looked out at him. It was just an ordinary boy's face, round and pale, with ordinary, flat, brown hair cut back firmly off the forehead. It looked like the face of a stranger. Peter stared at it. Was that really him?

'I've made a friend,' he told the mirror out loud, boastfully. 'His name's Jack Kimberley, and now he's my best friend.'

He stood up and gazed into the mirror beyond his own reflection. Part of his bedroom window glimmered in the background. He looked deeper. Through the window he could see patches of grey roofs sliding into the dips and niches of gardens and fields, and he could see the lane: the long, long lane stretching all the way to Juggins Wood. It took him by surprise. He stared harder. Yes, it was Juggins Wood in the very deepest reflection. Somewhere a glint of sunlight caught the lane as it crossed the water meadows, turning it to silver. His mind journeyed along the lane, into the wood, up the tracks, until he found the bubbling stream once more and found his own hideaway which he had called 'Peter's Den'. Somehow it was comforting to think that he could almost see it through his mirror, here in his own bedroom where he spent so much of his time. He stretched forwards and touched the glass, afraid to turn around in case it vanished away.

'Peter!' His mother's voice broke into his thoughts.

Obediently, Peter appeared at the top of the stairs.

'Mrs Brideworthy is going now. She would like to say goodbye to you.'

Mrs Brideworthy stood at the bottom looking up at him. She was swirled inside a long black cloak, making her look quite witch-like. She flung out an arm towards him as he came down.

'Goodbye, my dear Peter!' she exclaimed. 'It was enchanting to meet you.' Tentatively, he took her hand. Once more he was surprised. She squeezed it warmly, but it did not overwhelm him. She looked at him directly and her dark black eyes were friendly.

'The carrot cake was *delicious*!' she gushed. 'Thank you!' Then, with a whirl of her cloak, she swept out. Peter would not have been surprised if she had jumped onto a broomstick and flown away.

Her leaving left an empty feeling. Annabel turned sharply towards Peter. Instinctively he took a step backwards. Then he saw her face was flushed. She looked pleased.

'You can ride your bike if you want,' she said almost to herself.

For a moment Peter was taken aback. He had expected another big scene over the carrot cake.

'Just for fifteen minutes before bedtime,' she added.

Without a word, Peter fled through the door and out to the shed. His mother had made a friend too. A good friend, and somehow she had made the water flow under the bridge.

6
'Peter's Den'

Crystal flashing. Sunlight tumbling like gold coins. Dark long-fingered shadows creeping out from Juggins Wood across the green-gold stretches of water meadow. Dark specks of birds wheeling high on the wind, dipping and soaring like lost souls. Peter could see all this through his mirror, and he didn't dream that the very next day he himself would enter that scene. The very next day he would be cycling down that silver ribbon road and climbing the track through the woods.

It was all because of Mrs Brideworthy, spellbinder, witch extraordinary. She had taken Annabel away to an auction, leaving Peter in the charge of old Mrs Paget, their next-door neighbour.

Kindly and fussing, old Mrs Paget had given Peter his tea when he was brought home from school and, when he had finished his homework, urged him to go out with the others and enjoy himself. Then she settled herself comfortably in front of the television with her knitting.

It was with a strange feeling of freedom that Peter stepped out into the road with his bike.

A few of the children were riding up and down, but Jack wasn't with them. So he cycled down to Jack's house to see if he were home, but Charlotte told him Jack was playing a match with the school football team, and wouldn't be home for a while yet.

Peter stared down the road to Juggins Wood. As if in a dream, he found himself cycling down the ribbon lane, out of the village and across the water meadows. He imagined himself back in his room looking at his mirror image. It gave him a curious sensation to be in two places at once. He was both real and unreal at the same time, that was until he rode out of the reach of the mirror and into the sea-green gloom of Juggins Wood.

He hadn't meant to come, but here he was climbing the track as though he were sleepwalking. He would never be lost in this wood again. After all, it was his domain, his discovery, and a good king knows every nook and cranny of his kingdom.

When he reached the stream, he paused, his eyes sharpened as they scrutinised the muddy banks for signs of intruders. But he found none. The banks were undisturbed, and his stepping stones were just as he had left them. He smiled with contentment and turned towards his secret hideaway behind the hawthorn.

'Peter's Den'. The words still looked freshly scratched on the rock wall. Now he wanted to make his den more than just a crude shelter that any animal could crawl into. He wanted to furnish it, put possessions in it, items that occupied the space, staked a claim, and made it even more his own.

He wondered what he could secretly smuggle out and

carry on his bike? A cushion or two, perhaps? A blanket? A folding garden chair? It would be like camping. He could light a fire just outside the cave. He could cook, just as he and his father had done when they went camping together once.

So Peter sat at the mouth of his cave, like a caveman might have sat three thousand years before him, and pondered on the problems of shelter and warmth and food.

The hawthorn provided an effective screen and ensured his cave was completely hidden from view, but now Peter decided he needed a spyhole.

He felt for his penknife and fingered it for a while as he decided the best place to begin his task. Then he began, very delicately, to strip away a few leaves and twigs. The thorny bushes pricked and scratched his every move, but at last he succeeded in clearing a passage right the way through.

He stood back with a sigh of satisfaction. No casual eye would notice his handiwork. He crawled back to the mouth of his cave and tested the spyhole. He felt a surge of excitement. It worked. Now he could observe his territory and see without being seen.

For a while he stared through his spyhole. Then reluctantly, but still with a warm feeling of satisfaction, Peter crawled out of his hideaway and set off for home.

Much more quickly than before, he reached the track and half ran down the hillside. Just before he reached the bottom, he paused and looked into the trough of the valley. It was as though the ground was covered in snow as it was all white with wild garlic flowers, and the smell rose up to his nostrils, rich and cloying. He stared with some curiosity at the woods on the other side which climbed up and up to a spiky crest against the sky. It was like looking across the border into another kingdom, and he wondered about it.

Suddenly he had a strange feeling that perhaps he himself was being watched. He stepped instinctively behind a tree. He waited a few seconds then peered out cautiously. A wood pigeon flapped noisily out of the tree tops, but otherwise, nothing moved. Slowly he came out from behind the tree and carried on walking, but with his eyes fixed on the other side. He froze again, sure that something had moved. It was a hot still day; the shadows of the trees fell as solid and motionless as iron bars, so whatever had moved was not a branch swaying in the wind.

Uneasily, Peter walked on till he reached the shield of the next tree, then he crouched behind it and slid off the edge of the track down into the undergrowth. He lay silently watching. He saw it again. Someone was walking down the opposite track, someone who, too, seemed unwilling to be seen.

Now the figure was ahead of him, moving hesitantly, stopping every now and then to look, before carrying on towards the lane at the bottom.

Peter slid tentatively down the rough hillside, keeping under cover all the time. He knew both tracks met at the bottom to join the lane, and he decided to let the stranger arrive first. Just when he felt the figure was almost there, it disappeared from sight. Peter waited and waited, but no one broke from the cover of the trees and stepped out into the lane.

Peter was puzzled. Was the person waiting for him? Or was there another way out? He waited as long as he dared, but finally had to give up and carry on down to the bottom. Half-crouched, he quickly recovered his bike and heaved it out on to the lane. Then with a last furtive look round, he mounted up and cycled away as fast as he could.

As he rode, he thought about the mirror on his wall. It was as though it was waiting for him to cycle into its reflection. He pedalled faster. He could see the green stretch of the water meadows ahead and that was when his reflection would ride into his room. So taken up was he with the sound of his own wheels whirring along, that he didn't hear the sound behind him. Swift, like a swish of skirts, the sound was upon him.

Denis Corrie came out of nowhere. He lunged up against him on his racer, causing him to lose his balance and topple with a crash. Denis too squealed to a stop. He hurled his bike to the road and leapt on to Peter.

One knee was forced into his chest. Two hands gripped his head and forced it backwards.

'You little sneak. You little snobby sneak,' the voice spattered out. 'You've been following me, haven't you?'

Peter stared in horror at the fat red face which blazed over him. His eyes seemed to pop out of his head as Denis shook him up and down as if he were a rag doll.

'What did you see? Go on, tell me, or I'll bash your head in.'

'I don't know what you're talking about,' gasped Peter, barely able to get the words out between the shaking. 'I was just cycling down the lane. You must be mad. Lay off or I'll . . .'

'Or you'll what?' raged Denis. 'Call your non-existent daddy? Call your toffee-nosed mummy?'

Peter wriggled and fought bravely, trying to kick Denis away. But Denis was too strong.

'You've done nothing but sneak and spy ever since you came to our village. Tell me what you saw!'

'What could I have seen?' Peter insisted. 'I didn't see you till you jumped on me, you great bully!'

Suddenly Denis stopped shaking him up and down. He took a hand and squeezed Peter's cheeks so hard that tears came into his eyes. 'If I ever catch you spying on me, I'll get you. One way or another, I'll get you.' He stood up, panting. He kicked Peter's bike before picking up his own and speeding away.

Peter leant against the bank, dazed, and watched Denis diminish into the distance.

A voice hailed him. 'You all right, lad?' Percy Crimpwell pushed his pram out of the wood on a small path Peter hadn't noticed before.

'I'm OK,' Peter answered hoarsely, brushing himself down.

'I was coming along to help you,' Percy told him apologetically, 'but I was a bit far off to be of much use.' The old man came up to him puffing and looking guilty.

'That's all right,' Peter reassured him, but it made him wonder. Percy looked a bit afraid of Denis himself. His pram was stuffed with branches of wood and Peter could see the tip of an axe showing from underneath.

The old man hastily pushed it out of sight then said, 'Well, get along then, lad. Don't let me hold you up. I takes me time shuffling along.'

Stiffly, and with a throbbing head, Peter picked up his bike. 'Bye, Percy!' he called and slowly cycled towards the water meadows.

The sun dazzled him as he rode out of the gloom and into the wide brightness of the meadows. He looked towards the cluster of roofs within the village boundary and tried to identify his bedroom window. Opposite that window was the mirror on his wall and it would be looking at him now.

Old Mrs Paget didn't stir when Peter arrived home. He was glad she was asleep and couldn't notice his grazed knees where he had fallen and Denis's finger imprints on his cheeks. He crept quietly upstairs and stood in front of the mirror. Old Percy was pushing his pram towards the village.

Who had been in the wood on the other side from him, Peter wondered. Was it Denis? Or had it been Percy, secretly chopping down wood and hoping not to be found out? Well whoever it was, no one was going to stop him going to his hideaway. Kings had to defend their kingdoms, and he would defend his, somehow.

7
A secret
shared

In his dream, a fox stepped noiselessly through the wood. Not one leaf crackled beneath his velvet paws. Not one speck of light glimmered in his wild eyes. Yet Peter saw him through his spyhole. He watched his long low shape, like a moving shadow, slide in and out of the splashes of moonlight as he came nearer and nearer to the hideaway.

The fox reached the clearing and was about to step out into the open. Suddenly he froze in the very act of walking, one foot suspended in mid-air before him, his ears pricked as sharp as stars, his muzzle lifted. Slowly he turned and stared, and his stare seemed to burn through the darkness. He stared across the stream and the stepping stones, white as bones in the black water. He stared at the screen of hawthorn, penetrating its thorny spyhole. He stared straight into Peter's eyes.

Peter backed away into the cave, but the stare followed him, and a voice began to shout. 'How dare you spy on me! I'll get you for this!' It was Denis's voice. Then a huge shape hurled itself through the hawthorn into the cave. With a choking cry, Peter awoke. He sat upright in bed, gripping the blanket to his chin. It was as if the wood had invaded his room. Burst through the mirror. Roots and brambles, trees and fox – and Denis?

'I will not be afraid of Denis,' Peter said out loud in the darkness.

He heard a step outside his door. His cry had awoken his mother. Swiftly, he lay back on his pillow, silent and still, pretending to be asleep. The door opened. She listened, then went away.

'I will not be afraid,' Peter whispered again.

The next day, when Peter didn't appear in the road after school, Jack came looking for him. He crept through the hole in the hedge and sneaked across to the apple tree. Looking up towards the cottage, he could see Peter's bike leaning against the shed. Stooping low, he ran along the line of the hedge until he reached the shed window. He saw a movement inside and was about to flee, when he realized it was Peter. He bobbed up and tapped the window.

Peter looked startled, then delighted. He opened the window.

'I've found some brilliant stuff for the den,' he whispered excitedly. 'Come and see!'

Jack heaved himself on to the sill. For a moment, he see-sawed helplessly and they both got the giggles. At last, Peter grabbed him under the armpits and hauled him through, shushing and giggling and looking around anxiously in case Annabel should come.

'Look what I've found!' Peter pointed triumphantly to a

57

blackened old kettle, some grimy camping pots and pans, and several chipped aluminium mugs and plates.

'What's in here?' asked Jack, almost diving into one of the tea-chests. 'Hey! What about these?' He began hauling out old cushions and bedspreads over his shoulder.

Soon the floor of the shed was covered with all sorts of objects and materials so that it looked like a rummage sale.

'How are we ever going to get this lot to Juggins Wood?' asked Peter ruefully.

'Sssh! Your mum's coming,' hissed Jack, ducking down out of sight behind a tea-chest.

The shed door opened, and Annabel stood there, cigarette in hand and frowning.

'What the dickens are you doing?' she exploded, at the sight of the mess. 'Have you nothing better to do than create chaos in the shed? Just look at it!' She looked at the stuff on the floor which the boys had collected for the den. 'And as for that rubbish,' she said, 'tie it all up into that sheet and put it aside. I can see we need to call in the council to take it away.'

When she had gone, Peter and Jack tied everything up into the sheet as Annabel had said.

'What do we do now?' asked Jack.

'We'll get it to the den,' replied Peter firmly. 'The council isn't going to get this lot!'

'We'll have to make several trips,' said Jack. 'If I can take some of it to my house, it'll be easier.'

Like a pair of thieves, the two boys set about heaving the stuff through the shed window and dragging it to the bottom of the garden. From there, Jack took what he could through the gap in the hedge while Peter tied up the rest into manageable bundles.

It only took Jack three journeys, wobbling along on his bicycle, to transport all the bundles to his house. Then he and Peter sat beneath the apple tree and planned the next stage.

'What about Denis?' asked Peter. He managed to say the name quietly and with no hint of the panic he suddenly felt.

'What's Denis got to do with it?' Jack was puzzled.

'He beat me up yesterday. Said I was spying on him. Look!' Peter showed him the bruises on his arms and legs.

Jack winced with sympathy. 'Those Corries are a bad lot,' he murmured. 'They've had the police on to them many a time. Denis has been done for shop-lifting – and his cousins are worse. Watch out for Paul and Roland. You don't want to go nowhere near them. Course, they use Juggins Wood as a short cut to their pig farm at Whitham End.'

Granny Colston used to say, 'If you fall off a horse, get back on straight away before you lose your nerve.' Peter felt he must go straight back to Juggins Wood before nightmares and Denis and the Corries made him lose his nerve.

'Let's go to Juggins Wood today,' he said with sudden urgency.

'Can you?' asked Jack. 'Are you allowed?'

'I've done my homework, and I've tidied the shed. Mum said I could go out after I'd done that. I'll go and sort it out and see you outside your house. OK?'

His heart was beating fast as he ran back to the shed and Jack slipped through the hedge. He hurriedly thrust things

59

back into the tea-chests and pushed them into a tidy line, then he went into the cottage.

Annabel was watching television. He called out to her. 'I've done the shed. It's fine now, so I'll just be out in the road on my bike for a while.'

'No going into anyone's house,' said Annabel, 'and no accepting things from anyone, understand?'

'Yes, Mum,' replied Peter quietly.

'And mind you stay in the lane where I can see you . . .' she turned round to emphasise her words, but Peter had gone.

The two boys cycled side by side down the lane and out across the water meadows. Each had a bundle of mugs, plates and a cushion to take to the den.

As they rode, Peter fought with the fear of meeting Denis again. He couldn't help looking over his shoulder every few yards and glancing anxiously into the undergrowth. He knew they were still reflected in the mirror in his room, so he rode harder just in case, for any reason, Annabel might go into his room and see him riding to Juggins Wood.

He didn't tell Jack about the mirror. Not yet. Jack was being a knowall and not at all at his best.

'Of course, I come here all the time,' Jack boasted. As the road entered the shade of Juggins Wood, he remarked airily, 'Everyone knows these woods. We often have picnics here.' When they reached the clearing and Peter showed him where to hide the bikes, he said, 'I bet I'll know your den all along. I know all the good hiding places in this wood.' And when they began to climb the track he announced in a very casual voice, 'I've been up here millions of times.'

60

Peter said nothing, but just walked very fast. All his senses were tuned up. He wasn't listening to Jack prattling on, he was listening for the faintest sound – the crackle of a leaf underfoot or the flapping of a wood pigeon being disturbed by someone approaching.

At the bend in the track, Peter left the path and struck out into the rough. Jack fell silent. At last some of Peter's urgency and caution touched him. This was unknown territory for him. He didn't know every inch of Juggins Wood after all. He followed exactly in Peter's footsteps.

They reached the clearing. Peter paused before stepping out into the open. Every nerve in his body was sharpened to a pinprick, ready to pick up the slightest signal of danger. Jack stood at his shoulder, breathing heavily, feeling the weight of his bundle. Peter turned and looked at him. It was a strange look. It seemed to say, 'Can I trust you after all?' He could still turn back, still keep the hideaway his own secret.

The deep silence of a summer's afternoon hung over the wood. Everything was resting, peaceful. Jack waited and did not speak. Perhaps if he had spoken one word, if he had broken the spell, Peter would have turned round and gone back without showing him the den. But they stood together, breathing in rhythm, both listening.

Peter made the first move. He went forward into the clearing. 'Come on! It's over here.'

Jack followed slowly. He had been born and bred in Randall and had known these woods all his life, but he had never discovered this spot. Like Peter before him, he was filled with excitement. He rushed over to the stream and danced across the stepping stones. He dropped his bundle

61

of pots and pans to the ground and grabbed hold of one of the creepers to swing across the stream.

Peter waited in front of the hawthorn until Jack joined him.

'Where is it, then?' Jack asked looking mystified.

'We're standing right in front of it,' grinned Peter. He ducked right down and crept into the den.

Jack whistled with amazement. 'It's brilliant!' was all he could find to say.

There wasn't time for hanging around. Peter looked at his watch. 'Mum's programme ends in eight minutes. I've got to be outside my house by then.'

They unpacked their bundles and found a place for

every object then, just to make it feel like home, they sat down on their cushions facing each other.

'It's brilliant!' exclaimed Jack again.

'In about four weeks, it'll be the summer holidays so then I'll be able to come here – maybe spend the whole day,' cried Peter.

'We could bring food and sleeping bags. We could sleep here!' added Jack, as he saw the possibilities growing.

'I don't think I'd be allowed to do that,' shrugged Peter, 'but next time let's come with a torch, and matches, and sausages so that we can cook for ourselves.'

'What a den!' breathed Jack. He jumped up and ran deeper into the cave so that he disappeared into the darkness.

'We've got to go, Jack!' Peter called out. 'Come on out now!'

Jack reappeared, his eyes glittering.

'It goes on forever,' he gasped. 'We've got to explore. Next time I'll bring my dad's big torch, and we'll . . .'

'You'll keep it a secret, won't you?' cried Peter, suddenly alarmed at Jack's enthusiasm. 'Cross your heart, cut your throat, and hope to die.'

Jack looked him full in the eye. 'We're best friends now, aren't we? Course I won't tell. Cross my heart, cut my throat and hope to die.'

'We'll have to run all the way down, or I'll be late – and then I've had it!' said Peter bending down to crawl out of the cave.

Before he followed, Jack gave one last, thoughtful look round.

'You know what,' he pondered, crawling out into the

63

open. 'Your den would make a brilliant nuclear fall-out shelter. Really brilliant.'

Peter had been in bed asleep for about an hour when Jack's words came back to him and awoke him with a jolt. A nuclear fall-out shelter? Could they really hide from the bomb in his den? He remembered hearing that, if they dropped the bomb, the whole world would die. He felt a rush of terror. He put on his light, but it didn't comfort him. He got out of bed and crept to his mother's room. She was still awake, reading with her bedside light on. He stood in the half-open door, but she didn't see him. He longed to ask her questions like, 'If they drop the bomb, will we all die? Would Andy die in London, and Granny Colston too, would she die? What if the bomb dropped tonight?' He would never see them again.

Suddenly Annabel looked up and saw him. 'What are you doing out of bed?' she asked sharply.

'Can I get into your bed?' he asked in a small shaky voice.

'Really, Peter. You're too old for that now.' Annabel got out of bed. 'Come on,' she said softly. 'I expect you had a nightmare.' She took his hand and led him back to bed.

As she tucked him up, Peter said, 'Do you think they'll drop the bomb?'

Annabel frowned with alarm, then suddenly she bent down and kissed him.

'Of course not, Peter,' she said. 'Of course not,' and turned off the light.

8
An outing
with Dad

No one was quite sure when the hippies arrived. A battered bus with dents and scratches, painted in all the colours of the rainbow, was seen rumbling down the lane. The village shop buzzed with gossip because a girl with orange hair, wearing bright pink stockings and with a baby slung on her back, called in to buy some milk. Two young men, scraggy and unshaven with long, blond tangled hair and wearing earrings, were seen walking down the lane with a black mongrel on the end of a rope.

'Dirty devils!' snarled old Mr Ripley. 'To think I fought and nearly died in the last war for the likes of them.' Normally a placid, genial man, his cheeks went purple, and Mrs Ripley had to soothe him.

'Now, now, Bobby,' she clucked, 'they don't do no harm.'

Peter saw the two men and the dog. It was Saturday afternoon, and he was waiting impatiently at the gate for his father to collect him for the weekend. They gave him a friendly smile as they passed and the black mongrel jerked towards him with wagging tail and bright red, lolling tongue.

'What's his name?' asked Peter.

'Chaser,' answered one.

''Cos he's always chasing after something,' laughed the other.

Denis zoomed by on his racer, deliberately close.

'Oi! Watch out!' yelled one of the young men, drawing in the dog protectively.

Denis sped away with an insolent wave of his hand.

The two men sauntered on. They showed no anger, and Peter wondered where they were going.

Jack, Charlotte and the others came clustering round the gate.

'Did you speak to them hippies?' giggled Janet. 'I wouldn't go near them. You might catch something.'

'Look at their hair. I wouldn't like to put a comb through that. It's longer than mine,' squealed Michelle. 'And they never wash.' She pulled her face.'

'Where do they live?' asked Peter.

'In their bus, I think,' said Sean. 'Some of them have tepees. I went in one when some hippies came last year. It were great. Like Red Indians. They had a fire burning inside and the smoke went out through a hole in the top of the tent. It were great!' he enthused.

'Yeah!' snorted Gary. 'And you didn't half get into trouble back home. They camped on Mr Burgett's land and he called the police. By the time they came, the hippies had gone. They never stay long, but old Burgett said he'd shoot them next time.'

'I thought you were going out with your dad today,' said Jack.

'I am. He'll be here in a minute,' cried Peter craning over the gate to the top of the lane.

'You said that an hour ago,' Charlotte reminded him. 'Are you sure he's coming?'

'Of course I'm sure,' scowled Peter. 'It's a long way from London. He's probably been held up.' But, inside him, a seed of doubt was growing. It brought back memories of when they lived together. Andy was always vague; time meant nothing to him. He wouldn't know that Peter had had his overnight case packed for three days. He wouldn't realise that Peter had been too excited to concentrate at school that morning and had nearly got a detention. An hour late, two hours late – it was all the same to him. It wouldn't cross his mind that Peter had been waiting and waiting with despair growing inside.

Their heads jerked round at the sound of cheery beeping. A large, old, red estate car turned into the lane.

'He's here! It's my dad! I told you he was coming!' yelled Peter rushing out into the road. The car came to a standstill, and a tall gangly man, with floppy brown hair and wearing jeans, got out.

'Is Peter's dad a hippy too?' whispered Michelle.

'Don't be daft,' retorted Charlotte. 'You think anyone with long hair's a hippy.'

'Well!' Michelle studied him dubiously, as she watched Peter pitch himself into his father's arms.

Annabel appeared at the front door carrying Peter's overnight bag. She looked coldly at Andy. 'You're late,' she snapped.

'Sorry!' Andy gave Peter a shamefaced grin. 'Sorry, old man, I got held up!'

'You haven't changed, have you,' cried Annabel scornfully. 'You'd be late for your own funeral.'

Peter grabbed the overnight bag from his mother. 'Are we going now, then?' he shouted.

Andy looked at Annabel, wondering if she would ask him in. But she didn't. She just said, 'Make sure he's back by six tomorrow – sharp! And no excuses!'

'OK.' Andy shrugged and took his son's hand. 'Come on, then!' He turned to the car. Peter rushed after him, then suddenly stopped. He looked at his mother. She was still standing in the doorway, grim-faced, yet lonely. He took a step or two towards her.

'Mum!' he blurted.

'What's the matter now?' She sounded impatient.

'Will you be all right on your own?' asked Peter. Annabel's eyes met his for a second and softened. Then she said, 'Of course I will,' and shut the door.

The children had cycled off down the lane and were messing around as Peter got into the car. They waved good-naturedly as Andy drove slowly past. Jack held up his right arm like a Roman soldier saluting.

'One of your friends?' asked Andy curiously.

'My best friend,' replied Peter.

The road left the village and crossed the water meadows. They entered the leafy shade of Juggins Wood and Peter gazed up into the trees, trying to recognise the track he took. He didn't know why, but he felt no desire to tell Andy about these woods and the stream he had played in. They were too newly discovered to be talked about.

Suddenly, as they emerged on the other side of the wood, Peter looked back. He saw a thin coil of smoke rising up between the trees, floating like smoke rings into the blue sky. A wave of panic and fury gripped him. He gasped and leaned forward. Someone was in his wood. His wood. He wanted to shout to Andy to stop the car. He wanted to rush into the woods and up the banks to find whoever it was and tell them they had to go. How dare they!

'You're not going to throw up, are you?' asked Andy anxiously. 'Did you take a carsickness pill?'

'No,' replied Peter weakly. 'I don't get carsick. It's just . . . oh nothing. I thought I saw someone I knew.' He sank back and numbly watched the reflections of the trees bouncing off the windscreen as they went by.

'I'm taking you to my place,' said Andy, trying to make conversation.

'Are we going to Makepeace Avenue?' asked Peter. That was where they had all lived as a family once.

'No! We sold that. Didn't your mother tell you? I couldn't afford that on my own. Your mum needed the money – especially with her insisting you go to the nob's school like that – barmy, I call it!'

'I'd rather go to Jack's school,' said Peter.

'Your mate who I saw?' asked Andy. 'Yeah, well! She's got plans for you, your mother has. She just wants to see you do well.'

They drove on in silence. Peter felt his eyes getting heavier and heavier. By the time Andy hit the motorway, Peter's head had flopped on to his father's shoulder and he was fast asleep.

When he awoke, they were in the middle of London. Andy was changing gear at the traffic lights and loudly cursing a driver in front. Peter looked up, dazed. He had forgotten how big, bright and noisy the city was, where people flowed like rivers, and buildings soared high into the sky like glass mountains.

'Where's Makepeace Avenue?' asked Peter.

'The other side of town,' answered Andy. 'Miles away.'

'I wish we could go there. I wish we could all just live there together again.'

'Well, we can't, so put it out of your mind,' said Andy gruffly. 'It's over and done with.'

Peter remembered the water under the bridge and sighed.

They turned away from the bright lights and cruised down long streets of faded buildings. At last Andy stopped, cursing again because he couldn't see anywhere to park. Finally they eased into a spot and then walked up the road for a minute or so till they came to a building called Roseberry House. It would have once been a large family home when the kitchen was in the basement, the living-rooms and bedrooms on the first two floors, and the servants' quarters right up at the top. Now all the rooms were converted into flats. Peter could see people passing to and fro within the broad windows rather like figures which had come alive in their picture frames.

The building was white, but grubby. Paint flaked off the door and weeds choked the small front garden and all but blocked the basement window.

'Here we are!' exclaimed Andy, in a jolly voice. 'Hope you've got good legs – I live right at the top.'

The door opened into a bare hallway with dull brown lino on the floor and dusty, bare wooden stairs which seemed to rise endlessly before them. It smelt. Peter screwed up his nose and tried to hold his breath, but he couldn't for long, and as they started the long climb up the stairs, the trapped smell of stale food made him feel sick.

By the time they reached the second floor, Andy was breathing heavily and had to lean against the wall to catch his breath. Peter gazed at him curiously. He seemed a stranger now. He was older, fatter, and Peter noticed some grey hairs clustered round his ears.

'This'll be the death of me!' Andy joked. 'It's like climbing Everest every day.' They reached the third floor and suddenly it seemed cramped after the bare spaciousness of the lower floors. Andy took out another key and opened a door. He was wheezing heavily now, but as Peter stepped inside he managed to gasp, 'Welcome to my humble abode, Peter!'

Peter was stunned by the sight which met his eyes. The room was still in gloom because Andy hadn't drawn the curtains before he left that morning. Books and newspapers were scattered all over the floor; dirty cups and saucers, half-empty glasses of stale beer and ashtrays overflowing with cigarette stubs were tucked under chairs and tables, peeped from beneath the sofa and cluttered the mantelpiece. Andy's guitar was propped on a chair, the lead still plugged into the electric socket.

'Sorry about the tip,' said Andy casually, tossing Peter's bag on to a chair. 'Some of my mates came round last night and I didn't have time to clear up.'

'Mum would have a fit!' exclaimed Peter in a state of shock.

'Yeah! Well, she has fits about everything.' His finger stabbed a button on a transistor and Radio One blared out

defiantly. 'Help me tidy up!' yelled Andy over the din. 'It won't take long.'

Peter began picking up cups and saucers. Andy pulled back a rickety partition which revealed a kichen sink, a cooker and some wall cupboards.

'Stick them in here,' he cried.

Gradually the room cleared. Peter began to feel more relaxed. He looked out of the window and saw a forest of chimney-pots as far as the eye could see. He turned on the television, even though there was nothing to see. Annabel had banned television because she said he only watched rubbish. He looked around for the bedroom.

'Where do you sleep, Dad?' he shouted.

'On the sofa!' answered Andy. 'It pulls out into a bed.'

'That's brilliant!' exclaimed Peter, impressed. He'd never seen a sofa bed before. 'Do I have one too?'

'I suppose you can sleep in that one,' said Andy. 'I was going to put you on the camp bed, but I'll sleep on it if you like.'

Peter began trying to work out how to turn the sofa into a bed. He heaved and pulled and prodded, but it was no use. Andy laughed at him and then came over and did it in a flash. Peter leapt on to the bed and rolled around.

'Hey, Dad!' he yelled excitedly. 'You can watch television in bed!' He propped himself up on the cushions and stared at the screen flickering at the bottom of the bed.

'Course you can!' said Andy. 'That's the whole idea. I like my little luxuries, you know.' He flopped down on the bed beside Peter and the two of them lounged like kings.

'I like it here, Dad,' murmured Peter.

'Good,' said Andy. 'Here, take the remote control and find something to look at.'

Andy lay back and shut his eyes, while Peter flicked through the channels till he found some wrestling to watch. For a while they lay there contentedly.

'So this is your little nipper, is it, Andy?' A woman's voice cut through the noise of Radio One and the snorts and grunts coming from the wrestling on television. She had come right in and was peering mockingly at them over the top of the sofa bed.

Peter nudged Andy urgently. 'Dad! There's a woman!' But Andy's mouth had dropped open and it was evident from the gentle snores throbbing rhythmically that he was dead to the world.

9
The treat

The young woman winked at Peter as if they were old friends. She bent over and tickled Andy under his chin. He stirred and smacked his lips. 'Stop it!' he groaned, rolling over. She tickled him under the ribs, and this time he sat up annoyed. 'Oi! I said, lay off!' Then he saw her. 'Oh it's you. I might have known it.' He rolled sleepily off the bed.

'Well this is a fine way to take your son out for the day!' she teased. 'Aren't you going to introduce us?' She smiled coyly at Peter, who slid off the other side of the bed. He stared at her, not returning the smile. She looked so confident standing there in her tight black trousers, and vivid pink, baggy top.

'Peter meet Tanya. Tanya meet Peter,' yawned Andy.

'Hi, Pete,' said Tanya coming over to him and ruffling his hair.

She meant to be friendly, but Peter shook his head away from her hand and stepped back in a wave of hostility. Who was she to walk in as if she owned the place? To call him Pete, when everyone else called him Peter and to look at Andy in the way she did, as if they belonged to each other?

'Cat got your tongue?' cried Andy, irritated. 'Say hello to Tanya.'

'Hello,' muttered Peter with lowered eyes. 'Dad, shall I help you put the bed back into a sofa?'

'You won't be able to manage it,' replied Andy brusquely and he heaved it back into place himself.

'I'll make some tea,' said Tanya cheerily going behind the partition. 'Did you like the bike, Pete?' she called out.

Peter looked puzzled and turned to Andy. 'Does she mean the bike you gave me, Dad?' he asked.

'Yeah!' he nodded. 'You've got Tanya to thank for that bike. It used to belong to her little brother. He's too big for it now so she said you could have it. Wasn't that kind of her? Of course, I had to clean it up. Right state it was in,' he added.

Peter felt confused. 'I wish you'd told me. I thought you'd got it for me.'

'What difference does it make?' said Andy lightly. 'You got a bike now and I hope you're having a good time with it – eh?'

'Yeah, Dad! It's great. Thanks,' said Peter, though the lack of enthusiasm in his voice made Andy heave a sigh of impatience.

'Well, say thank you to Tanya. You owe it to her.'

'Thanks, Tanya,' said Peter.

'What?' shrieked Tanya from behind the partition. 'Do you really need the telly on as well as the radio?' she cried. 'I can't hear a thing.'

Andy switched off the television and turned down the radio.

'What did you say, love?' Tanya asked Peter as she came out with a mug of tea.

'Thanks for the bike,' said Peter simply.

'Don't thank me, love. I suppose you should thank my kid brother, Jimmy – but then since his gran gave it him, I suppose you should thank her,' and she burst out laughing.

Peter didn't know whether he felt better or worse about it. He just wished it had been Andy's gift alone.

'We thought we'd take you to the zoo, didn't we, Tanya? You'd like that, wouldn't you, pardner?' said Andy, suddenly becoming jovial and giving Peter a slap on the back.

'Yeah!' murmured Peter, though his heart sank at the word 'we'. He wanted to say, 'Dad, I'll go with you. Send her away, and I'll go anywhere with you.'

'You don't sound too keen,' grunted Andy.

'Of course he's keen!' soothed Tanya. 'All kids love zoos! Don't they, Pete?'

Peter didn't reply. He knew he would much rather lie on the sofa bed for the rest of the afternoon, watching television, and if they did go to the zoo, he didn't want to go with her. He scowled.

Andy and Tanya exchanged glances, then Andy said, 'Come on, then, Peter. Let's go and get the car. See you downstairs, Tanya!' He pushed Peter through the door. Half-way down the stairs he stopped and faced the boy furiously. 'You little blighter!' he stormed. 'Don't you go all toffee-nosed with me and my friends. I suppose that mother of yours thinks everyone's beneath her! I thought those private schools were supposed to teach you manners.

77

That's why I live in this pigsty, to help pay for that school of yours, so don't you dare go all snobby on us.'

Peter stared up at his father with horror. 'I wasn't being snobby, Dad, honest!' He felt the tears rising up in his eyes. 'I just . . .'

'Oh, don't start snivelling,' Andy snapped impatiently. 'Just be a bit more friendly.' He ran on ahead down the stairs and was out of the front door before Peter reached the bottom.

Miserably, Peter stood on the front steps while Andy brought the car to the front. He got out and held the door open.

'Get in!' He indicated the back seat with a curt nod of his head. Peter got in and sank into a huddle. 'Where's Tanya? Doesn't she realise I'm double parked?' Andy grumbled.

The front door opened, and Tanya appeared at the top of the steps. She called out to them. 'I've been thinking. You two don't see that much of each other. I think you should go on your own. I'll stay back and tidy the flat – it's filthy!'

'Come off it, Tanya!' protested Andy. 'We want you to come, don't we, Peter?'

Peter didn't answer, but inside he was shouting, 'No, no, no! Leave her behind, Dad. Let's just be you and me.'

'I've made up my mind,' said Tanya firmly. 'Have a good time and I'll see you later.'

Andy heaved himself into the driving seat and slammed the door. Peter could see his father's scowling face in the rear-view mirror. He started the car and shot off too fast and had to squeal to a standstill at the traffic lights. Then suddenly he caught Peter's eye. Andy winked, and Peter grinned. He leaned forwards on the driver's seat.

'Dad!' he said cautiously. 'I'm hungry, Dad.'

Andy struck his head and exclaimed, 'Of course you are. Sorry, old chap, I'm not used to hungry kids any more. You must be starving. Shall we eat first or find something at the zoo?'

'Can we have a hamburger?' asked Peter. 'Mum never lets me have one when I'm with her.'

He must have known that was the right thing to say because Andy immediately said. 'Of course you can. Right away.'

The zoo was forgotten. Peter was glad; he hadn't wanted to go anyway. They found an American Hamburger Bar, and both ordered half-pounders with everything on it. They sat in leatherette booths at shiny, yellow plastic tables, sipping from glasses as big as vases full of frothy chocolate milk shake, and gazed through the huge plate glass window at the world streaming by.

For a while they ate in silence. Peter sank his teeth through the soft white bun. The tangy juices overflowed and trickled down his chin. Like mirror images of each other, he and his dad dabbed their mouths with their paper serviettes and picked up their hamburgers for the next big bite. As they both opened their mouths wide, they caught each other's eye and paused. It was the first time they had fully looked at each other. They stared at each other, mouths still open, then Andy grinned and put down his hamburger.

'Doing all right at school, then?' he asked.

'OK,' shrugged Peter. 'Trouble is, I'm not much good.'

Andy looked cross. 'What do you mean, not much good. Who says so?'

'I only come sixth or sometimes seventh in the class,' said Peter glumly.

'We can't all be top!' laughed Andy encouragingly. 'I used to be bottom.'

'Yeah,' sighed Peter. 'But unless I come at least in the top three, I'll never get the scholarship. Mum'll kill me.'

'Oh no, she won't,' snarled Andy. 'She'll have to deal with me first. When do you take it?'

'Next April, but I wish I didn't have to.' They carried on munching for a while, pausing to dab their mouths and suck the thick creamy milk shake up through their straws.

'Still playing the fiddle?' asked Andy. He never used the word 'violin', always 'fiddle'.

'I'm taking my grade two soon,' said Peter. 'My violin teacher says I'll pass.'

'Well there you are!' Andy thumped his shoulder. 'You

see? Everyone's good at something. Perhaps you'll be a musician like me! Now, how about an ice cream?' Without waiting for an answer, he leapt to his feet.

'Dad! I couldn't!' Peter protested. But Andy had already joined the queue. The ice cream was a double, topped with cream, chocolate sauce and nuts.

'Here you are, pardner!' cried Andy putting it before him with a flourish. 'Let no one say that I don't look after my little boy, eh?'

Peter gazed doubtfully at the mountain in front of him. He knew that every inch of his stomach was full.

'Dad . . .' he began hesitantly. 'I don't think I can manage all this.'

Andy shifted with annoyance. 'For heaven's sake! Why did you ask for it then?'

'I didn't . . .' Peter's voice trailed away when he saw the exasperation on his father's face. He dabbed the top of it with his spoon and licked it.

Andy looked at his watch. 'I've got to make a 'phone call,' he said. 'Have that finished by the time I get back.' He made his way out of the hamburger bar and disappeared into the crowds to look for a 'phone.

For a few moments Peter swirled it round with his spoon as if hoping it would somehow melt away. But if anything it looked more and, no matter how many little licks of the spoon he kept giving, nothing seemed to make it look any less.

Then he noticed the clown. It was a big, yellow, plastic clown standing nearby in baggy blue trousers, with arms outstretched and a broad red mouth. Written across his chest were the words, 'Fill me'.

Peter glanced around, but no one was looking at him.

He slid out of the leatherette booth and looked around again. Still no one took any notice of him. He picked up his ice cream, and with a final guilty glance, dashed over to the clown and tipped it through the wide, smiling, red mouth.

10
Will they
drop the bomb?

Far away across the city a police car sped. It's siren wailed, changing key as the car rushed through the night.

Peter lay awake, his eyes open. Here in London it was never dark, never quiet. He remembered now. The lamppost outside filled the room with an ugly, murky, orange glow. He decided now that he preferred the dark, even though the dark made him worry.

'Dad?'

Andy grunted.

'Are you awake?'

'I am now.'

'Do you think they'll drop the bomb?'

'Course not.'

'But if they do, what will we do?'

'Oh, go to sleep, can't you?'

'What will we do if they drop the bomb?' Peter persisted.

'I dunno. Nothing. Nothing we can do.'

'Couldn't we go into a fallout shelter?'

'There aren't any. Not for the likes of us, anyway.'

'If there was a fallout shelter in Randall, would you come into it?'

'Don't suppose there'd be time. They only give you a four minute warning.'

Peter fell silent, thinking about that problem. Four minutes. That wasn't even enough time to cycle from Trimble Cottage to the hideaway.

'Dad?'

There was no answer, just a long low snore.

The next morning Peter awoke first. He had now got into the habit of waking early whether he banged his head or not.

The first thing he thought about was the den. Jack was right. It would make a good fallout shelter. He'd heard of secret shelters deep inside mountains. This one went into the hillside, too. They hadn't yet discovered how deep. The problem was the four minute warning. How could Andy get there in time?

He looked at his father. He was still sound asleep and didn't look as though he would wake for hours yet. Last night Tanya had cooked supper for them, then she and Andy had talked and smoked long into the night. Peter had watched television until his eyes began to close, stinging with smoke and fatigue. Finally, Tanya had noticed and made Andy put him to bed. He was put into the camp bed, much to Peter's disappointment, but Andy and Tanya were sitting on the sofa, and that was that.

Peter got out of bed and dressed. Tanya had gone. He stared out of the window into the empty Sunday morning street below.

'You up already?' Andy groaned in a muffled voice.

'Dad! You should come and live in Randall,' urged Peter.

'Your mother would love that,' muttered Andy sarcastically.

'We ought to live closer in case they drop the bomb.'

'Peter!' Andy rolled over and sat up in annoyance. 'Are you still thinking about the blooming bomb? For heaven's sake! No one's dropping the bomb and I'm not moving to Randall.'

'But . . .' Peter began.

'That's enough . . . enough, do you hear? Now let me get a bit more shuteye, will you? If you're so wide awake, go and get the Sunday papers for me and a comic for yourself. There's money in my pocket and the key to the front door.' Then he flopped back and pulled the duvet right over his ears.

Peter was pleased to leave that stuffy room, smelling of beds and tobacco. He stepped out into the street and breathed in the fresh air. The newsagent was only on the corner, but Peter didn't hurry. He walked along the pavement carefully avoiding the cracks. 'Step on a crack and you break your mother's back,' he chanted quietly.

He stopped to stroke a cat who followed him along a low wall, leaning its body against his hand and purring like an engine.

At the newsagent, he browsed over the comics first. Annabel never let him read comics. Even in the dentist's waiting room. Now he poured over them avidly, hoping the lady behind the counter wouldn't notice him too soon.

'Come on, sonny!' she said at last. 'This isn't a reading

85

room. Them comics are for sale. Can't have you putting your dirty fingers on them all. Either buy one or scram.'

Peter chose a Captain Marvel comic about him saving the world from nuclear destruction, then he bought Andy's Sunday paper too.

Andy was still asleep when he got back to the flat. Peter spread the Sunday papers out over the floor and searched for any news of the bomb. The rustling finally woke his father. He yawned loudly and squinted at his watch. Then he stumbled out of bed and out on to the landing where the lavatory was.

Peter was afraid he might go back to bed again, so when he came in he said, 'Dad! What are we doing today?'

'We're having lunch with your gran.' He went behind the partition and turned on the electric razor.

'Granny Colston? Oh good!' cried Peter jumping up.

'Glad something pleases you!' yelled Andy over the sound of the razor.

'Is she coming too?' asked Peter.

'Who's she? The cat's mother?' demanded Andy, turning off the razor.

'Tanya!' said Peter reluctantly. He didn't like saying her name.

'Tanya!' repeated Andy heavily. 'No. Tanya is not coming.' He started up the razor again.

'Good,' muttered Peter.

'What did you say?' yelled Andy.

'Nothing!' shouted Peter. 'I'm glad we're going to Granny Colston's.'

Andy came out washed and shaved, and Peter got his overnight bag together.

'I wanted to sleep on the sofa bed last night,' complained Peter, as Andy tossed the duvet cover, pressed it down and folded up the bed into a sofa.

'Yeah, well, another time,' replied Andy lightly. 'We'll be carrying on back to Randall after Granny Colston. So make sure you take everything with you.'

Peter tucked his Captain Marvel comic down the side and made sure his pyjamas covered it completely. He wished he'd bought a chocolate bar now. He was starving and it didn't look as though they were going to have any breakfast.

His starvation increased as they walked up the path to Granny Colston's door an hour later. It brought it all back: Granny Colston's kitchen full of warm, delicious smells of baking or pickling or roasting and simmering.

The door flew open, and Peter found himself hugged till he could hardly breathe.

'It's been a long time, Peter!' she cried, holding his face between her hands and studying him.

It had been a long time. Peter ran from room to room like a puppy dog, sniffing and touching and checking that everything was the same as he remembered. The carpets were still fluffy, the curtains flowery and the furniture still smelt of lavender polish. The little china ladies with their crinolines and parasols still posed on the mantelpiece, the silver desk calendar, with a knob that you turned to change the date, was still on the folding desk in the corner and, best of all, the shining brass animals which Grandma collected were still clustered round the grate in the fireplace.

Andy did what he always did. He settled himself into a deep, cushiony, easy chair and began to read the papers.

87

'Granny, I'm starving!' gasped Peter, following Granny Colston into the kitchen.

'Grate these carrots for me,' she said, handing him a grater, 'then you can eat one. Lunch won't be long.'

'Gran?' Peter scraped the carrot carefully.

'Yes, dear.'

'What will you do if they drop the bomb?'

'Good heavens! What a question. They're not going to drop the bomb, dear,' she laughed.

'Everyone says that,' frowned Peter, 'but what if they do?'

'I'll hide under the kitchen table!' she teased.

'Gran! Be serious. This is important. You should be prepared.'

'What is a little head like yours bothering about the bomb for?' asked Granny Colston looking worried. 'There's nothing we can do, so there's no point in losing any sleep over it.'

'Are you anywhere near a nuclear fallout shelter?' asked Peter.

'There's the old air-raid shelter at the bottom of the garden. Trouble is, it's all filled in.'

'I didn't know you had an air-raid shelter in your garden!' gasped Peter excitedly. 'Where is it? I can't see it!' he cried, craning his neck to see out of the kitchen window.

'See that rockery at the bottom of the garden?' Gran pointed. 'It's under there. Ugly thing it was too, so we turfed it over and grew flowers on it. Now you'd never know.'

'Did you ever go in it?' demanded Peter in a thrilled voice.

'Oh yes. Quite often. Especially when them awful doodlebug things came over. I'll never forget the night this house was hit.

'Was it?' gasped Peter. 'I can't see anything.

'It's all put back together now, but that day – it was a warm summer day – like today really. We were sitting in the kitchen – right here round the table. It used to be in the window before we got that worktop. A friend had given us a huge bowl of cherries. I still remember how bright and shiny and fat those cherries were. Some of them were dangling in twos or threes and we hung them round our ears like earrings. Suddenly, the air-raid sirens went. What a noise! It still chills my blood when I hear the factory sirens go. Just like that it was. We grabbed blankets and pillows and ran. I wanted to take the cherries too, but I was rushed away too fast. We went into the shelter. Horrible place really. Dark and dank and smelly. We sat there all huddled up, listening to the bangs and bumps outside, and then we heard the really big bang – so big our shelter shook and bits of it fell in, and we all thought we were going to be buried alive. Then everything went quiet. It seemed ages before the siren went again to tell us it was all clear. When we came out, what a mess! Half the house was gone. All the windows had been blown in and right where we had been sitting was just a gaping hole.

'But the most amazing thing was, that there, in the middle of the rubble, in the middle of the kitchen that had no walls or roof, there stood our kitchen table, and on the table was the bowl of cherries. I remember how red they looked in all the dust and confusion.'

Peter finished grating one carrot and began to munch it. 'You could dig it out.'

'Dig what out?' asked Granny puzzled.

'The air-raid shelter. Then you could use it again if they dropped the bomb.'

'Shouldn't think it would be much use against H-bombs,' sighed Granny. 'H-bombs are a different kettle of fish.'

Andy came in. 'When are we going to eat? I'm starving.' And Peter didn't ask any more questions.

By the time they had had lunch, cleared it up, washed up and played a game of cards together, it was time to set off for Randall.

As they were leaving, Peter put his arms round Granny

Colston's neck and whispered in her ear, 'Come and live in Randall. You'll be safer there.'

'You just take care of yourself, my lad,' smiled Granny giving him a kiss, 'and perhaps this will help you along.' She pressed a five pound note into his hand.

Peter carefully zipped it up into his jacket pocket. That was another thing Annabel mustn't see. She'd only go and put it into his savings.

He and Andy didn't say much to each other on the journey back. It seemed a long drive and Peter felt a lump of misery growing inside him as they got nearer. He wanted to beg Andy to stay. He didn't want him going back to that poky room in London. He didn't want him going back to Tanya.

Suddenly there they were, driving through Juggins Wood. Peter looked anxiously for the smoke he had seen when they left. But there was no sign of life anywhere. No sign of old Percy, or Jack, and no sign of Denis Corrie. They reached the edge of the water meadows and Peter knew they were driving into his mirror and into his room.

'I won't get out,' said Andy as they pulled up outside Trimble Cottage. 'It only upsets your mother. Keep your chin up, OK, pardner?' He spat in the palm of his hand and held it out.

'OK, pardner,' said Peter. Without smiling, he spat in the palm of his hand and clasped his father's.

The next time they met, Peter vowed he would have the den so organised as a fallout shelter that he would show it to Andy. He was sure Andy would then see how sensible it would be to move to Randall, just in case they dropped the bomb.

11
The hippies
get the blame

Odd things began to go missing in Randall. Mrs Sidley lost her purse with everything in it. 'I left it on the kitchen table with my shopping. I must have only been upstairs for a minute but when I came down, it was gone.'

'The same thing happened to me,' cried Mr Runcorn. 'I put a ten pound note on the table, ready to pay the coal man. I was only in the garden, pottering with me dahlias. The coal man arrives. I goes to pay him, and bother me! The money's gone.'

'Could it have blown away?' suggested Mr Hamley. 'Did you have a really good look?'

'I put the teapot on it,' retorted Mr Runcorn indignantly. 'It couldn't have blown away. Nope. Somebody walked in – in full daylight, cool as a cucumber – and took it.'

'What a nerve!' Mrs Paget shook her head in amazement. 'We'll have to start locking our doors,' said Mrs Sidley tight-lipped. 'Things are getting as bad as the city.'

'It's all these types coming into the village. Outsiders.

Take those hippies. If I had my way, they'd all be in the army. That would soon sort them out.'

'You don't think they. . . ?' asked Mrs Runcorn looking shocked.

'You're too soft on people, Mrs Runcorn. These people aren't the same as us. They have different standards. Different morals – I mean, look how they let their children run round naked. It's disgusting!'

'That doesn't make them thieves,' Mr Hamley pointed out.

Peter was in the village shop buying a list of groceries for his mother. When he got home, he told her what he had overheard.

'Come to think of it,' Annabel frowned in thought, 'I'm missing something too. I'm sure someone's been into the shed. That stuff you put aside for the council to take away – well, it's gone. I suppose I ought to report it to the police.'

Peter felt his face go bright red. He turned away hurriedly and began to stack the groceries in the cupboard.

'Perhaps a tramp took it,' he said.

'More likely to be those hippies,' declared Annabel. 'People like that don't believe in property. They think everything is theirs for the taking. But you notice they have nothing to give in return.'

'I don't see why the hippies should get the blame,' said Peter quietly. 'It could be anyone.'

Peter was desperate to find Jack. What if Annabel did go to the police? What if they went searching through Juggins Wood? What if they found out about the den? He didn't want the hippies to be blamed, but he couldn't tell about the hideaway.

Peter pushed his bike cautiously out into the road. He peered warily up and down, ready to dodge out of sight if he should see Denis. But the road was empty. Peter cycled to Jack's house.

He saw Charlotte first.

'Hi!' she said with a friendly smile. 'Here, can you hold Jacob for me while I clean out his hutch?'

Peter took the animal awkwardly. He wasn't used to handling pets. At first it scrabbled in his arms and stuck its claws in his jumper, and Peter nearly dropped it. Then suddenly, it found the crook of his arm and snuggled in quietly. He stroked its silky head and long ears.

'What a nice rabbit,' he murmured, rubbing his nose in its fur.

For a while he watched Charlotte meticulously tipping out the old straw into a black plastic bag and scrubbing the inside of the hutch to make sure it was absolutely clean. Then she spread the new straw so that it lined the hutch like deep wall-to-wall carpeting, popped in some nice fresh carrots and chopped apple, and refilled his water bottle.

'There!' she said stepping back with a satisfied sigh. 'Now you can put him back inside, if you like.'

Charlotte held open the door of the hutch, while Peter bent himself towards the opening. The rabbit leapt from his arms and immediately began nibbling at the apple.

'Where's Jack?' asked Peter looking around. 'Is he home?'

'Probably watching telly,' replied Charlotte. 'I'll go and find him.'

Peter hung ouside the front door and Mrs Kimberley saw him. 'Hello, Peter. Come on in!'

Peter hung back. 'I'd better not, thanks,' he said politely. 'I'm not allowed to.'

'I've just made some nice fairy cakes,' said Mrs Kimberley. 'I'll go and get you one.'

'Er . . . no thanks . . . thanks a lot . . .' stammered Peter trying not to be rude. 'I've just had my tea, so I mustn't.'

'I can see I shall have to go and see your mother and formally invite you to tea,' she laughed.

Jack appeared with his mouth bulging with fairy cake. 'Go on, Peter. Have one,' he begged. 'They're fantastic!'

The warm rich smell had already begun to weaken his will. It reminded him of Granny Colston's kitchen, so he finally gave in and said, 'OK.'

'We promise not to tell,' teased Charlotte.

Peter dragged Jack outside. 'My mum might call the police!' he announced dramatically.

Jack looked at him wide-eyed. 'Why?'

'That stuff we took to the den, she thinks the hippies stole it!'

'Why should she go to the police?' cried Jack. 'She was throwing the stuff out anyway.'

'Other people have had things stolen too,' explained Peter. 'I heard them in the shop and they're all blaming the hippies.'

'Do you want to put the things back?' asked Jack.

'No! She'd guess I had something to do with it. I'm just worried about someone finding our den, especially if it's going to be our nuclear fallout shelter.'

'Yeah!' agreed Jack. 'Then everyone will want to come

in. We've got to keep it a secret.' He chewed his cheek and frowned in a worried sort of way. 'I wonder where their bus is? I haven't seen it for a couple of days.'

Peter remembered the coil of smoke he had seen rising from the trees on his way to London. He looked in despair at Jack. 'I'm sure they're somewhere in the woods.'

'We ought to go and check. Shall we go now?' Jack suddenly looked excited.

'I can't,' groaned Peter. 'It's far too late. I must be going right now.'

'I'll go on my own, just to check.'

'What if Denis is there?' Peter said doubtfully.

'He wouldn't dare hurt me. My dad sorted him out once before,' replied Jack confidently.

'What are you two whispering about?' Charlotte had come creeping up with a sly grin on her face.

'M.Y.O.B.' snorted Jack.

'What's that?' cried Peter, mystified.

'Mind Your Own Business!' Jack said.

'Are you up to something, Jack Kimberley?' asked Charlotte suspiciously.

'M.Y.O.B.' repeated Jack stubbornly. 'Come on, Peter. I'll ride to your house with you.'

The two boys cycled off, leaving Charlotte staring after them thoughtfully.

'I wish I could go with you,' sighed Peter, as he said goodbye and wheeled his bike up the path. 'Be careful.'

'I'll be all right. I'll go like an Indian: silent as a snake, invisible as the wind!' he exclaimed dramatically.

Silent as a snake, invisible as the wind. Peter liked that. He repeated it to himself as he got ready for bed. From time to time he gazed into his mirror hoping to see some sign of Jack on the road to Juggins Wood, but under the darkening sky the road ran long and lonely. Annabel came in and drew the curtains tightly together. Peter got into bed and lay back on the pillow. She kissed him briefly and said good night.

He felt helpless, imprisoned, lying there thinking about Jack roaming free. Silent as a snake, invisible as the wind. He thought about slipping out of the house and cycling swiftly away to Juggins Wood, but tonight Annabel was still up, moving restlessly around. No matter how hard he tried to stay awake, she was still up when his eyes closed and he finally surrendered to sleep.

Later, much later, it was a miracle he awoke. It was a miracle Annabel didn't wake up. There was a sound as sharp and as brief as a pistol shot. Peter thought he was dreaming and half woke up. Then there was another shot. No, not a shot, an object striking the windowpane. He leapt out of bed and rushed to the window. He peered through the darkness into the garden below. A bright beam of light hit him between the eyes. As quietly as he could, he pushed open the window and leaned out.

'Pssst! Peter! It's me, Jack! Come down, can you?'

Peter didn't risk a reply. He waved a hand then drew back quickly. He went to the bedroom door and listened. Nothing stirred. He found his torch from under the pillow and, trembling with excitement, crept downstairs.

Jack was waiting by the kitchen door as Peter slid back the bolt and stepped outside.

'Let's go in the shed,' whispered Peter.

They felt safer inside and the boys balanced their

torches on the tea chests. In the narrow beams of distorted
light and leaping shadows, Peter looked at Jack's face and
was shocked.

'What's happened? Is it the den? Has someone found it?'

'I'm sorry, Peter. I'm really sorry. I couldn't help it!' Jack
mumbled, almost in tears.

'What's happened? What are you talking about?' Peter
cried fearfully.

'It's . . . I know I promised . . . but . . .'

'It's my fault,' said a voice in the doorway. Charlotte
moved into the beam of torchlight. 'I know about the den.'

12

Preparing
for the bomb

Peter looked at the two of them: brother and sister, white-faced and serious.

'I promise not to tell,' whispered Charlotte. 'Jack was so upset about it, he couldn't sleep. He wanted you to know right away. So in the end we decided to sneak out and come and tell you.'

'I had to show her the den. We had to hide, see? There was nowhere else to go,' stammered Jack.

Peter listened to their story with sadness. Juggins Wood was no longer his. It never had been.

'I cycled to the wood, just as I said I would,' Jack continued. 'I was a little way up the track when I heard voices, so I ducked down and hid in the bushes. I'd have been all right if it hadn't been for her.' He looked accusingly at Charlotte.

Charlotte shrugged without repentance. 'It's not my fault. I saw you cycle off like a bat out of hell. I knew you two had a secret of some sort, so I followed. I saw Jack turn off into the woods, but by the time I arrived he'd vanished.

I was looking around when suddenly I saw the Corrie Gang. They were all there – Denis and those cousins of his. Paul Corrie had his scrambling motorbike. What could I do? I couldn't go home, knowing Jack was somewhere in there with those Corries messing about.'

'You should have just hidden for a while until they'd gone,' cried Jack angrily. 'But oh no, you have to start calling me!'

'I only called you softly,' retorted Charlotte. 'Anyway, I had to find you.'

'Yeah! Well of course they heard. Then all hell broke loose.' Jack scowled at his sister. 'You should have just minded your own business. Paul got on his motorbike and rode down to the entrance. He was shouting something about those hippies being around and how he'd have their guts for garters!'

'The other two were carrying some bags or something – and that was really strange. They kicked them into the bushes as though they were hiding them,' said Charlotte. 'That's when I thought, "I bet they're up to no good," so I hid too. I knew they hadn't seen me, but they were looking. I was really scared.'

'So was I!' added Jack. 'I was terrified. Then Paul began roaring up and down the paths, swerving in and out of the trees. Once, he came so close to me, I thought I'd had it. The others came down and blocked the entrance out on to the road, so you see, we could only go up.'

'I was getting cramp in my leg where I was all crouched up,' Charlotte went on. 'I tried to straighten it, but I fell over. The others heard me and yelled. I panicked and began to run.'

'I began to run too – up towards the stream.' cried Jack. 'The Corries never saw us close enough to know who we were, I'm sure, but they were yelling and shouting and all of them began chasing after us.'

'That's when we saw each other,' said Charlotte, ruefully. 'Jack hissed, "Follow me," so I did. My leg was really hurting. I was limping along. It was awful. I could hear the motorbike coming up behind us.'

'The den was our only chance, Peter,' said Jack, his eyes pleading with him to understand. 'Paul knew we'd gone into the rough. He couldn't follow on his bike, so he went on up to find another way round. That was our chance. I know they didn't see us. I dragged Charlotte into the den – and that was it.'

There was silence. They both looked at Peter, wondering how he was going to react.

'I saw your name scratched in the rock; "Peter's Den",' said Charlotte softly.

After a while Peter said, 'You're sure they didn't see where you went?'

'Positive!' said Jack firmly. 'They didn't come anywhere near.'

'We could hear their voices all round and that motorbike revving up and roaring about, but then they gave up and went away,' added Charlotte. 'I could hear them blaming the hippies, but we didn't see any sign of them at all.'

'Everyone blames the hippies,' sighed Peter. There was more silence.

Then Charlotee said, 'Well, we'd better get back before anyone finds our beds empty.' She pulled Jack's arm, and indicated the door with her head. 'I promise not to tell. Ever!'

Peter looked at her closely. 'Cross your heart, cut your throat and hope to die?'

'Cross my heart, cut my throat and hope to die!'

'Spit in your hand and shake on it,' ordered Peter.

Charlotte and Peter shook on it.

'That makes you one of us . . . one of the brotherhood . . . or sisterhood . . . or something, doesn't it, Peter?' Jack's eyes gleamed with relief.

'Yes,' said Peter solemnly. 'That makes you one of us.'

They stood for a few moments, shoulder to shoulder, united in the feeble beams of their torches. Then Charlotte and Jack moved towards the door of the shed.

Before they stepped out into the darkness once more, Charlotte turned. 'Oh . . . and Peter . . . don't worry about anyone finding your den. Even if the police went searching through the woods, they'd never find it. It's too well hidden.'

The three of them separated each to their own bed and to sleep. Once more in his room Peter stood at his window looking towards Juggins Wood. In the midnight sky, the moon struggled like a lonely swimmer. Clouds ráced over its surface, first drowning it completely, then lifting it up so that its face bobbed clear and moonbeams fell across his bed. The night was disturbed but Peter felt calmer. One thing he knew for sure: he was not at all upset about Charlotte.

Summer came upon them with a rush. Suddenly the woods were lusher and deeper, the trees leafier, the bushes

102

thicker. Little paths and tracks, if they weren't used often enough, got swallowed up. The hideaway became more hidden.

With each visit the children made to it they took something with them for the den. They now had a cushion each to sit on, a small table, a mat to cover the earthy floor and an old curtain to sling across the opening of the cave.

With each visit they looked for new paths and approaches to the cave, trying to make sure they were never seen or followed.

Charlotte said they should have a warning call so that they could communicate with each other without using their voices in the woods. Jack and Charlotte knew how to blow an owl call. Peter didn't.

'First cup your hands like this,' Charlotte demonstrated. She folded the cupped left hand over the cupped palm of her right hand. Her fingers were tightly closed together but left a hollow in the middle. 'Then you put your thumbs together and bend them at the knuckle, like this. Now, see this little gap between the thumbs? You blow through it like this.' She put her lips to her thumbs and blew. A low hollow sound, just like an owl, escaped from her hands.

Jack cupped his hands and pranced all round the clearing hooting. 'It's easy peasy,' he boasted.

Peter blew and blew cupped and uncupped his hands, but he couldn't get out any sound but the sound of his own breath.

'I know!' cried Charlotte, seeing Peter was getting upset. 'Use a blade of grass. That's just as good.' She ran on to the slope beyond the waterfall where tall flat-bladed grasses wavered purple and green. She picked several blades, judging their flatness and thickness, and brought them to Peter to try.

'Look! Like this,' Charlotte stretched a blade between her two thumbs and blew on it. A high piercing shriek echoed round the wood.

'That doesn't sound anything like an owl,' commented Jack, disparagingly.

'Yes, it does. That was the owl's hunting cry. It's just like that,' retorted Charlotte. 'Now listen.' She found another blade and stretched it between her thumbs. She blew again, but a little more gently. The blade of grass quivered and a low throbbing hoot floated into the air.

'Let's have a go!' cried Peter excitedly. He succeeded almost immediately. 'I know! Let's use the hooting sound when we are apart but want to get in touch secretly, and the warning sound when there's danger, like somebody coming!'

'Yeah!' agreed Jack with wholehearted enthusiasm, and they all ran off in different directions practising their calls on each other.

Somehow Peter felt the wood had become theirs again, even though he knew the Corries could be up the track on the other side, even though he knew the hippies could be camped somewhere deeper in the wood. The hideaway was so hidden, he felt safe, and at least the kingdom of the little clearing was their own.

Best of all, Charlotte thought the idea of using the den as a nuclear fallout shelter was very good, but said they would have to do a lot to it before it would be any use.

'We have to think of storing enough food for each of us to eat for up to three weeks,' said Charlotte.

'I'll save my crisps every day from my packed lunch,' offered Jack.

'Crisps won't be much use,' said Charlotte. 'We'll have to bring in cans of baked beans and things like that.'

'Brilliant!' exclaimed Jack. 'I could live off baked beans forever.'

'I couldn't,' murmured Peter.

'I'll bring macaroni chesse and spaghetti hoops,' said Charlotte. 'What about you, Peter?'

'I'm not sure,' said Peter. 'I'll have to look and see what Mum has.'

One tin here, one tin there, would anyone notice? Mrs Kimberley didn't seem to. For Peter it was harder. Annabel's cupboards were meticulously ordered and arranged. Even when Peter shuffled all the other tins a little bit closer to close the gap, he felt sure Annabel would notice the gap at a glance.

In any case, Jack was scornful. 'What's this?' he jeered, holding up one of Peter's contributions. 'Artichoke hearts! Ugh!' He grabbed another and read the label. 'As . . . para . . . gus . . . tips? What's that?'

'I dunno,' admitted Peter. 'I just took it because there were two of those tins.'

'I'm not eating as . . . para . . . gus tips or artichoke hearts,' declared Jack.

'You will if you're starving,' Charlotte told him squarely. 'People eat rats and worms if they're starving.'

The cave began to get crowded. Charlotte decided to start piling tins down the tunnel at the back of the cave. She crawled in deeper and deeper with her torch, discovering little niches to stack things in. At first it seemed

the tunnel would get too low and narrow to go any further, then suddenly, as she flashed her torch, Charlotte found it got wider again.

She told the boys about it. 'We could use it for the toilet,' she said.

'What!' The boys gave a shriek of disgust.

'If we can't go out for three weeks, then we've got to have somewhere to go to the toilet,' argued Charlotte patiently. 'We've got to think of it like being in space for three weeks.'

'Oh no!' groaned Peter. I suppose that means we've got to bring in three weeks' worth of toilet paper.'

'If the bomb dropped, just supposing,' asked Jack in a quietly reasoning voice, 'and we come here to our shelter . . .'

'In four minutes!' added Peter. ''Cos that's all the time we'll have. . . '

'What will Mum and Dad be doing?' Jack looked worried as he spoke.

'We haven't really thought who's coming here,' frowned Charlotte.

'I've got to bring my gran and my dad . . . and Mum,' said Peter firmly. 'I've just got to.'

Jack pitched in. 'And we've got to have our mum and dad, and Charlotte won't leave her rabbit, will you, Charlotte? And there's our gran too . . . and . . . '

'Oh shut up, will you!' Charlotte burst out. 'We've got to decide properly. I mean there isn't room for everyone.' She looked upset.

Jack scrambled out of the cave at top speed before anyone could stop him.

'I'm going home!' he muttered vehemently.

Peter and Charlotte followed him as he raced across the clearing and plunged into the trees.

'Jack!' Charlotte called impatiently. 'Don't go off in a sulk. It's only a game, you know.'

Peter looked at Charlotte in amazement. 'Only a game? I thought we all believed it. All the plans we've made – was it for nothing?'

She shrugged with an awkward grin. 'Well . . . my dad says they'll never drop the bomb.'

13
Running
away

The bomb did drop. It dropped a few days after Peter had broken up for the summer holidays. It dropped the day his school report landed with a thud on the mat.

He was upstairs in his room, waiting. He knew his report was due today. He heard the click of the gate and the postman coming up the path. He heard the shuffle of letters through the letter box.

Annabel was down in the kitchen. She had taken two weeks off work to look after him, then he was due to go to Andy's for two weeks. He heard her footsteps going to the front door. He pictured her exactly as she bent down and picked up the long, white, heavy envelope. He saw her taking the letters to her bureau in the living-room and opening up the long, white, heavy envelope with her antique ivory letter opener.

He sat on the bed stiffly, waiting. He didn't know how many minutes went by. It could have been hours or years. Then she called him from the bottom of the stairs.

'Peter!' How could one short name contain so much anger in it?

He went slowly to the top of the stairs. They stared at each other. She held the report up in her hand.

'Get down here!' Her voice shook with anger.

He walked down the stairs, holding the bannister as if for comfort. As he reached her, she struck him.

He hardly heard what she said. A torrent of words poured from her mouth. He was lazy, useless, ungrateful. She had sacrificed everything for him, worked herself to the bone to pay for his fees. For what? To come all but bottom in the class? To get no mark higher than a B? It was Andy's fault; she raged on about 'that father of yours'. It was the children's fault, always hanging round the gate distracting him. Most of all, it was the bicycle's fault. If it hadn't been for that bike, he would have concentrated more, spent more time on his homework. 'Do you see now why that bike has to go?' she raged.

He stumbled back up to his room and lay on the bed trembling. He heard the front door slam shut. He heard the shed door being opened and the whirr of wheels as she took his bike down the path.

A few minutes later, the car started up. He didn't try to see. She was gone. The bike was gone.

He sat up, her voice still ringing in his ears. His heart was thumping strangely fast as if he'd been running, yet his brain was clear and his eyes were dry.

He didn't know what made him decide to run away. Perhaps it was when he took the mirror off the wall and re-hung it with its face to the wall. His limbs unstiffened. He began to move rapidly. He dragged his overnight bag out from under the bed, even before he had planned what he was doing. Once started, he began to move quicker. He stuffed the bag with pyjamas, sweater, socks and pants. He remembered how he and Andy used to go camping together. He even remembered a towel, soap and toothbrush. He pulled out a knapsack which was stored in a cupboard. Inside was his sleeping bag, neatly rolled. He tried to remember what was still needed. Torch! He would need his torch. He felt for it under his pillow and stuffed it in the bag. He was going to the hideaway, of course, so he needn't worry about food. There were plenty of tins to keep him going – for weeks if need be. Tins! Tin-opener! Mustn't forget that. He raced downstairs and rummaged through the cutlery drawer. Toilet paper! He raced back upstairs again and stuffed a roll into the knapsack. Anything else? Money? He had Granny Colston's five pound note still zipped into his anorak pocket and his post office book was in Annabel's bureau.

As he fumbled through the bureau looking for his post office book, he began to panic. She might come back. He had to go. Suddenly there it was: the bright blue book. He snatched it from the drawer and pushed it into his pocket.

He straightened up, knapsack on his back and overnight bag in hand. He opened the kitchen door and went down the path.

The lane was empty. He wished he could leave a note for Jack and Charlotte. They were still at school for at least another week. But they would know and would be sure to come to the cave.

He studied the lane again. Who might see him? Stop him? Question him? If he took the route past the post office and the village shop, dozens of people might notice him. He must take the long route round to Juggins Wood, even if it took him hours, so he turned in the opposite direction.

Running, then walking, Peter took the old bridle path through Badham's Yard where the children liked to play. He scrambled through the weeds and in and out of the derelict buildings of what was once Badham's Mill. Here he found a track which climbed steeply up a bank and emerged in the high grazing fields surrounding Randall Village. For a while he let the path take him where it wanted, but at last he found himself on a ridge overlooking the lane below and the water meadows. For the first time he paused, his chest heaving and his arms aching with the overnight bag. He was now pointing in the direction of Juggins Wood.

Peter knew all the approaches to the hideaway. Cautiously, he took a longer, rougher route which brought him out on the rocky slopes above the cave. It was a steep clamber down, hanging on to thorny bushes, slithering down from one foothold to another. But at last he arrived. With a cry of relief he stumbled inside. It was nearly an hour since he had left home. Sliding out of his knapsack, and dropping his overnight bag to the ground, Peter fell exhausted on to the cushions and immediately went into a deep sleep.

Outside the cave the day moved on from morning to afternoon and then into evening. Peter slept, awoke, cried a little and slept again.

An owl hooted. Peter stirred, half-awake. It hooted again, a little nearer. Peter sat up excitedly. Could it be Jack? Or Charlotte? He cupped his hands and tried to hoot a reply, but though he blew and blew, he could not make a sound.

Suddenly, the curtain across the mouth of the cave moved as a hand drew it carefully aside. Two anxious faces peered in at him.

'You look awful,' said Charlotte bluntly, studying Peter's tear-stained, mud-smeared face. The three of them were sitting solemnly in a circle on their cushions.

'I've run away,' confessed Peter sheepishly.

'I know. Your mum's been looking everywhere for you.'

'You haven't told anyone I'm here, have you?' Peter gripped Charlotte's arm.

'Of course not!' she reassured him.

'Fancy running away! You lucky thing!' breathed Jack enviously. 'Why don't we run away, Charlotte?'

'Shut up, Jack,' snapped Charlotte. She looked at Peter who had dropped his head in his hands. 'What are you going to do?'

'I'll live here. No one will find me. There's plenty of food, I'll be fine. I might go to London. Go to my gran's, but that will be later. If I go now, they'll only send me back. I could stay here forever.' He looked at them both, trying to explain. 'She hates me, my mum. I never do anything right. I'm no good at school. That's why she got mad. My report came today. She took my bike away.'

'You poor thing,' Charlotte put her arm round him sympathetically. 'But you ought to go home, Peter. Your mum's quite upset. She might call the police if you're not back by tonight.'

'I'm not going back!' Peter pulled away angrily. 'And you won't tell anyone, will you? You promised. Remember? Cross your heart, cut your throat and hope to die.'

'Course she won't tell,' said Jack fiercely. 'I'll kill her if she does.'

'Will you come and see me every day?' asked Peter hopefully.

'We can't!' cried Charlotte. 'Jack and I are going on a school trip for two days. We're leaving tomorrow.'

Peter hung his head with dejection.

'Will you change your mind and go home?' asked Charlotte gently.

'No,' answered Peter.

Jack leaned closer to his friend. 'I'll bring you back a present. Something nice, OK?'

Peter nodded, unable to speak.

'We'd better go, then,' said Charlotte reluctantly.

Peter nodded again.

'I won't tell, I promise,' she said.

'Here!' Jack rummaged in his pocket. 'Would you like this?' It was half a Mars bar.

'Thanks!' said Peter taking it from him.

When they had gone, Peter stood staring after them for a long, long time. Then he ate the Mars bar. It made him feel better, but terribly thirsty. Drink! They had never thought to bring any drink. He went to the stream and cupped his hands under the water bubbling out of the rock. As he drank, he remembered: if they dropped the bomb, all the water would become radioactive and undrinkable.

A blood red sun slipped like a burning ship beneath the rolling surface of the hillside. Black rooks rose cawing and splattered themselves like ink smudges across the dark blue sky. Peter was hungry. He opened a tin of baked beans. He hated them cold. Tomorrow he would light a fire.

He unrolled his sleeping bag, spreading it as far back from the mouth of the cave as he could. Then he crawled inside and slept.

He awoke once in the pitch darkness and thought he heard his name being called from a great distance. But sleep rolled him over once more and carried him on through the night.

14
Menace
in the wood

Peter awoke slowly because he didn't want to wake up. He lay with his knees drawn up almost to his chin and his head tucked down into his sleeping bag. He looked like a caterpillar inside its chrysalis waiting to be born.

A pang of hunger made him groan. The open tin of baked beans was on the table nearby, the spoon still in it. He reached over and ravenously consumed a few spoonfuls. This time he didn't care that the beans were cold. Then he wriggled back inside his bag, not yet ready to face the world.

The sun moved round as the day progressed. A bright shaft of sunlight penetrated the gloom of the cave. It drew him out. He crawled to the entrance and peered through his spyhole. The clearing was empty, yet sparkling with life. The stream wriggled with reflections; birds skimmed over the tree tops and plunged between the bushes; insects darted across the surface of the pool.

For many hours Peter hung around the cave just sitting and staring into space. He felt sometimes numb, sometimes frightened, sometimes stubborn, but mainly angry. Whenever he thought of Annabel driving away with his bike, all thoughts of going home died. He did feel lonely.

Only once he left the clearing to go and stand like a ghost at the edge of the water meadows. The long empty road ran towards Randall. It would run past his house. He only had to follow it. He knew that if the mirror were hanging face outwards he would be reflected in it, standing in his own room. But he had turned it in, so for the moment his room didn't exist.

Even before darkness fell, Peter crawled back into his sleeping bag. His thoughts were jumbled with terror. He could hear rustles and scratchings and murmurings which seemed to surround and enclose him. Here he was in his kingdom, but was he king or fox? Hiding or seeking? Somewhere out in the woods, a dog began barking. Peter remembered the hippies. The thought that they were close by, that they too were sleeping out in the woods comforted him. Tomorrow he would try and find them.

Now that he had given himself an aim, something to look forward to, Peter relaxed and slept dreamlessly.

The next day when Peter awoke, he felt different. He felt brave and he didn't feel lonely. He found his soap, toothbrush and toothpaste and washed himself in the stream. It made him think that if the hippies were camped somewhere in the wood, they would surely be near water. He decided to follow the stream, climbing upwards into the areas of the wood he had not yet explored.

He stuffed his pockets with two packets of Jack's crisps and waded along the stream with his shoes hanging round his neck by their laces.

It wasn't always easy. The ground was rougher and steeper. The stream sometimes fell through narrow gullies and Peter had to put on his shoes and make a detour round before catching up with it again.

The sun was powerfully warm. Peter took off his shirt and tied it round his waist. He had stopped to rest on the bank and was practising owl calls through a blade of grass when he heard the sound of a machine. At first he thought it might be an aeroplane. Then it came nearer. Peter just had time to roll out of sight as a motorbike hurtled past.

Peter had only ever heard of the Corrie Gang. He had never seen them, but somehow he knew this must be one of them. Perhaps the one who had chased Jack and Charlotte. He crouched in the undergrowth fearfully, wondering what to do, which way to go. Then he heard another sound. It was even more disturbing. A high-pitched scream, very faint and very thin. Peter was sure it was a human cry. It came from somewhere ahead of him. Keeping to dense undergrowth, Peter stalked through the wood like the fox in his dream. Each step he took, one in front of the other, was measured and carefully placed. At the faintest sound he stopped to watch and listen. There was silence. Peter thought the motorcyclist had gone when, suddenly, his heart nearly leapt through his mouth with the shock. There he was, only a yard or two away, sitting powerfully astride his black and white machine.

Peter recoiled in horror, but he hadn't been seen. The rider was staring intently at something down in the dip. The sharp silver studs on his jacket glinted dangerously as he reached out and clutched the handlebars. He jumped on the starter and squeezed the throttle. A deafening roar filled the woods, and a cloud of blue, evil-smelling fumes billowed into the air. Machine and rider turned and pointed themselves down into the dip like a weapon. Peter thought he heard the scream again, but he couldn't be sure over the din of the motorbike.

The machine pushed off. Peter leapt forwards to the edge of the dip and lay flat in the long grass watching. The rider plummeted to the bottom, swerved in a circle and climbed up the other side.

As the blue smoke cleared, Peter saw the child. He was very young, perhaps five or six, and he stood there quite naked, clutching a bunch of wild garlic in his hand with his mouth wide open for another scream. The machine had raced off along a track. It seemed to go a long way and then suddenly there was silence again.

The silence was mocking, as if the rider were playing with the child, building up his fear. In that silence, Peter took his chance. He slithered down the dip holding his hand out to the boy.

'Come here! Quick!' he hissed.

The boy clutched his hand and Peter dragged him over into the undergrowth. He remembered how Jack had said the motorcyclist wouldn't go into the rough, so he dragged the child through the bushes and brambles to get as far away from the scrambling track as possible.

Once again they heard the kick of the engine. Peter pulled the boy down into a bush and they lay gasping and stinging with the scratches on their bodies. The machine roared over their heads to the top of the dip. They heard the engine ticking over as the rider paused and looked below him. Then they heard his puzzled threatening shout.

'Hey! Hippy! Where've you gone? Think you can hide from me? I'll find you, you little rat.'

The boys didn't move a muscle.

'I'm coming, hippy!' The engine was switched off. Silence again. 'I'm coming to get you!' the voice sang softly. The boy opened his mouth as if to scream again, but Peter pressed his hand over it tightly. They could hear the rider's footsteps breaking heavily through the undergrowth. Peter tensed himself up for discovery, when suddenly there was the roar of a second engine.

Another rider appeared at the top of the dip. 'Hey! Paul! Watcha doing?' he called.

The first rider stopped and retraced his steps through the undergrowth.

'Chasing hippies!' he laughed.

'Aw c'mon! Let's go! The gang are waiting for us at the farm.'

The first rider climbed the slope to his machine. He swung astride. Before he kicked the starter, he yelled, 'We'll be back, hippies! So you'd better watch out!'

Peter waited till the sounds had completely died away before getting to his feet. The little boy was crying quietly.

'Where do you live?' asked Peter.

'Over there!' The child waved his hand towards the upper reaches of the wood.

Still clutching his bunch of wild garlic, the child led Peter on and up until, quite suddenly, the wood ended. Before them a grassy hillside rolled away and folded itself into other hills and valleys, on and on into the distance.

Peter smelt the wood smoke before he saw the tepee. He had found the hippies.

15
With
the hippies

The tepee was just as Gary and Sean had described.
It was very big, much bigger than an ordinary tent. A swirl
of heavy canvas was strapped to the top of three or four
poles, then fell out cone-shaped and fixed at intervals into
the earth. But the twins hadn't said how beautiful it was.
The canvas, though faded, was painted with huge yellow
circles like suns inside blue triangles. There were white
moons and stars and a great brightly coloured rainbow
which swooped down from top to bottom.

Three or four children ran around, some naked, others
in shorts or skirts. They looked grubby, their hair matted,
their faces streaked, but they laughed and squealed with
such pleasure that Peter longed to rush out and join them.

The child he had rescued raced towards them waving
his clump of garlic and calling strange names, 'Freya, Pim,
Ollie, Tara!'

A flap in the tepee was tossed back. Was it a girl or a
woman who came out in a long flowing skirt? She lifted the
child on to her hips and smothered him with kisses.

The smoke spiralled up from a wood fire a few yards from the tepee. A tall young man stoked the flames. He looked like a warrior with his bare chest and long, flowing, blond hair bound by a headband. He stirred a round, metal, cooking pot which hung from a home-made spit over the flames and, all the while, the black mongrel Peter had seen being led through the village bounded about, sniffing the smells and slapping his chops with his long, red, lolling tongue.

'It's Chaser,' thought Peter. 'They call him Chaser because he always chases after things.'

'Hey, Seth! When's food!' the children called.

'Now!' shouted the warrior good-naturedly. 'Come and get it!'

Two more women emerged from the tepee, and it seemed to Peter that a tribe of people wandered over to the fire. The children gathered up bowls and spoons and held them out in turn, while Seth ladled steaming portions into each one. Peter felt a fierce hunger.

Suddenly the flap of the tepee was thrown back again. 'Still more people?' thought Peter. A man appeared and immediately Peter felt there was something different about him. He was older, thin, almost wizened. He had long, black, tangled hair which hung round his shoulders, and a black beard sparkling with silver strands. He didn't look like a warrior, but there was a power about him in the way he moved. It was as if he were a magnet; everyone turned towards him, even the dog. The children clustered round him, and, as he approached the fire, they all made room for him.

The strange man went over to the cooking pot and took

123

the ladle from Seth. He bent and said something to one of the boys. The boy turned and looked in Peter's direction. Then he started to run towards him. On and on he came. Peter couldn't believe it. How did they know he was there? He wanted to run, but couldn't. It was as if he were held under a spell. The boy came right up to the edge of the trees where he was hiding, then stopped.

'Hello, Peter,' said the boy softly. 'Vikram says will you come and join us? You must be hungry.'

Too amazed to speak, Peter stood up and silently followed the boy across the field to the fire. Friendly faces smiled at him and the little boy he had rescued came to his side and took his hand.

Vikram looked at Peter with black merry eyes and, with a soft piping voice, said, 'Welcome, Peter. Come and sit and eat with us. You must be lonely.'

Tonight the summer sky would never turn black, even by midnight. It would stay rich and dark blue though the sun went down and the moon and stars decorated the sky like those on the tepee.

No one asked him questions, they just welcomed him, smiled at him and fed him. When the eating was over, Peter played with the children. He got to know who was Ollie and Freya, Pim, Kikkha and Tara. They took him inside the tepee and he saw how they lived and slept and how, in winter, they could light a fire inside and the smoke could escape through the hole in the top.

'Have you ever lived in a house?' asked Peter.

'Some of us have,' said Ollie. 'But we don't like houses. We like to be free. We like sleeping outdoors whenever we can, being on the move. If we find a nice place, we stay; if we don't like it, we move on.'

Peter wanted to know who belonged to whom – who were brothers and sisters and who were mothers and fathers. They just laughed and said they were all brothers and sisters to each other and the grown-ups were mothers and fathers to them all. No, they didn't go to school. The grown-ups taught them – especially Vikram. No one knew more than Vikram.

Yes, it seemed Vikram did know everything, even things it didn't seem possible he could know. Peter watched him from time to time, fascinated by him. Once he caught his eye and he cocked his head like a bird, as if watching and listening to things other people couldn't perceive.

Later, a soft tiredness descended on the camp. No one said, 'It's time for bed.' The children just played and played until, one by one, they were overcome by sleep and crawled away into the tepee to bed.

Seth drew out a wooden flute and curious melodies rose into the night air. Sometimes the others joined in singing, or else just talked quietly, the flames of the fire casting shadows over their faces.

Vikram sat a little apart staring intently into the fire. Peter came and sat next to him and he, too, gazed into the embers. They created so many pictures. He saw Andy and Granny Colston and Annabel too. Was it the wood singing as it burnt, or did he hear them calling his name with sad voices?

'Your mother wants you to go home,' said Vikram gently.

'She hates me. I'm no good,' Peter answered huskily.

'No good?' echoed Vikram. He flung an arm upwards and pointed to the glittering sky. 'Would you say any one of those stars was no good?' he demanded.

Peter stared at the wide star-filled universe.

'You are like one of those stars. Different, special, unique. There is only one Peter Colston in the whole universe and that's you. You are more than good. You are precious.'

'I wish my mum thought so,' murmured Peter.

'She does. She loves you,' insisted Vikram. 'She just doesn't know how to show it. Some people never learn to show their love, but it's there, crying aloud inside them.'

Peter didn't speak.

'Your father and grandmother, they're very worried about you too.'

Peter looked at Vikram. 'How do you know? How do you know?' he exclaimed in amazement.

Vikram simply shook his head mysteriously. 'They want to see you, Peter.'

'I want to see them too,' Peter burst out. 'I want them to come and live round here. I've been making a nuclear fallout shelter so that if ever they drop the bomb we can all hide away and be safe in my cave. But they won't come and anyway there's not enough room, especially if Jack and Charlotte bring their mum and dad and granny, and Charlotte's rabbit and . . . and anyway . . . there's only a four minute warning. What can we do in four mintues?' Peter wept.

'Ah!' sighed Vikram. 'The bomb. If they drop the bomb, even if your shelter was ten times bigger and deeper, do you really think it would save you? You can't stay in it forever. One day you'll have to come out and then what will you find? A poisoned world? Don't hide away, Peter. Come out now while there's so much to live for.'

Peter was silent except for his weeping.

'We live close to nature.' Vikram waved his hand to indicate the camp and the woods and the low rolling hills all around. 'So long as nature lives, we live. If nature dies, what right have we to live?'

'Can I live with you?' asked Peter. The warmth of the fire thickened his voice and dried his tears. He leaned drowsily against Vikram and fell asleep without waiting for an answer.

When Peter awoke he was back in his cave and the sun was already high. He didn't remember coming back to the hideaway. Perhaps after all it had just been a dream – the hippies, the fire, the tepee. Had Vikram been a dream too?

Peter walked down through the woods to the edge of the water meadows. As before, he stood looking at the long road which could lead him home. If the mirror had been facing the right way round, he would be home, but he didn't know if he was ready to go back. He went on standing.

Mrs Brideworthy too was standing and thinking. She and Annabel had come into Peter's room. Annabel felt closer to him here. Ever since he had run away she had come again and again hoping to see some sign that would tell her where he was.

At first she had been angry. She felt it bubbling up inside her, choking her. How dare he hurt her like this. How dare he humiliate her, after all she had done for him, all the sacrifices she had made. Then she realised how much she missed him and her anger turned to an ache of despair. If only he would come home, she would try and be a better mother. 'I promise to try,' she said out loud.

Mrs Brideworthy patted her comfortingly. 'I'm sure he's not far away,' she said. 'I can feel it in my bones.' Once again, she examined every detail of Peter's bedroom. His books, toys, furniture. Then she stared out of the window. She looked without really seeing. Something bothered her. She turned and saw the reversed mirror opposite her on the wall. She frowned.

'What's this?' She lifted the mirror off the hook.

'Peter liked it', said Annabel listlessly.

'I wonder why it was hung with its face to the wall?'

puzzled Mrs Brideworthy. She replaced it on the hook with its face turned outwards, then stood back looking at it. She didn't just look at it. She looked through it, beyond her own image, beyond the reflections of his room and out through the window. Now she saw the long grey road running like a ribbon out of the village and across the water meadows. A large grey heron lifted its body out of the marshy ground and flew a low flight path towards Juggins Wood – and then she saw him. Peter. He was standing there like a sentinel, keeping watch. Two figures came into view and blocked him from sight just for a second, but when they had passed Peter had gone.

Peter heard voices and stepped back into the trees. The two figures Mrs Brideworthy had seen came along the road, arguing fiercely. Peter dropped to his knees and kept perfectly still.

'You be the one, ain't yer?' It was Percy Crimpwell's voice. 'I figured it were you all along, but now I know,' he went on, his voice rising. 'You and those rotten cousins of yours, it's you that 'ave been stealing from the houses and blaming it all on the hippies.'

'You can't prove nothing!' sneered the other voice. It was Denis. Peter tightened into a ball, hardly daring to breathe.

'Anyway,' Denis jeered, 'who are you to talk? We all know where you get that wood. And is that a power saw I see tucked down in your pram? Tut, tut! I could get you into trouble; cutting down wood – that's nicking, too. You been thieving since before I was born!' His voice was triumphant.

Percy grunted angrily. 'You whippersnapper. The law'll catch up with you one of these days. You'd better watch out. They're all over the place now, looking for that Colston boy. Let's hope you had nothing to do with his disappearance.'

'Me? Why you . . .' Denis lunged towards the old man in a fury. 'Do you think I'd touch that creepy little snob? I hope they never find him! And you'd better stay clear of the Corries. OK?'

'Well, I expect the thieving will stop, will it, now that the hippies have moved on? I seed their battered old bus going off early this morning,' Percy sniffed.

'Yeah!' Denis boasted. 'We put paid to that lot, we did! And we'll put paid to you too, if you meddle.'

The voices separated as the two went their own ways; Percy on towards the village, Denis up the track towards Corrie's pig farm.

16
Losing
and finding

Peter clawed his way out of the ditch and ran. 'No! No!' The word pounded in his brain as he scrambled, slithered and clambered up the stream through the woods. 'Please let them be there! Please don't let them be gone!' His lungs were almost bursting with pain as he reached the green fields where the hills rolled away into the distance. 'No! No!' he cried out loud. 'Pim! Ollie! Tara!' He called out the names of the children. 'Vikram!' His voice echoed hopelessly round the empty field.

It hadn't been a dream. The remains of the camp fire were black and smoking where they had been trampled over. The tepee lay dragged and ripped across the field. Motorcycle tracks scarred the yellow suns in the blue triangles; knife slashes tore through the moon and stars and the brightly coloured rainbow. It hadn't been a dream. They had sat together round the fire. For one evening he had been a part of them and now they were gone. Driven away. Peter felt abandoned.

131

'Look! There's another of those hippies!' A harsh voice bellowed across the field. 'Let's get him!'

Peter saw Denis running towards him with malicious pleasure. The blood rose before his eyes. Misery gave way to fury. He rushed towards Denis like a wild animal, and flung himself at him, punching and kicking.

'It was you!' he screamed. 'You did the stealing. You drove them away! I'll kill you!' The two boys fell to the ground struggling and pummeling.

'Get him off me!' yelled Denis. There was a roar of motorbikes. Peter felt rough hands dragging him off his enemy. Someone gripped him by his hair and pushed his face backwards, another gripped his chin and squeezed till the tears came into his eyes.

'What shall we do with him, the dirty little hippy?'

Denis got shakily to his feet, then gasped with shock. 'Let him go, Paul!' he panted. 'It's Peter Colston! He's the one the police have been looking for.' There was stunned silence. Peter felt the grip on his chin loosen, then he was hurled to the ground. 'Leave him! Come on, let's get out of here.'

Denis jumped on the back of one of the motorbikes and, with a thunderous roar, they revved up and were gone.

Peter lay like a fallen soldier on the battlefield. He could hear crows cawing in the distance as if bewailing the violence they had witnessed. He huddled griefstricken, unable to move. He wished he were dead.

Suddenly he felt a warm, wet, slurping tongue licking his cheeks, his neck and snuffling hot breath down his ear. Peter rolled over with a cry of delight. 'Chaser! Chaser! They left you behind too!' He got to his knees and hugged the dog almost to death. Chaser leapt all over him, licking and barking.

Peter looked round the field and the fringes of the woods. Surely they couldn't be far? They would never leave Chaser. But he saw nothing except the black crows wheeling round in the sky and the desolate field.

He gave Chaser a comforting pat. 'Never mind,' he said. 'You can come home with me.'

Chaser stayed close at heel as Peter led the way downstream to the hideaway. He and the dog crawled inside and Peter collapsed exhausted on to the cushions, while Chaser sat patiently at his side.

He lay with closed eyes and felt as if he and the cushion rose up and up and floated away. He was floating over the woods and marshy water meadows. There was the long grey road running into Randall. There was Trimble Cottage and his mother looking up into the sky as he floated past. She waved, but before he could wave back, he had floated on. Now he was over London, almost bumping into the tall glassy builings where clouds drifted in the windows. There was Andy parking his car. He shouted to his father, 'Dad! Dad, I'm here!' But Andy didn't hear him, he sprang up the steps and into the flats. Then Peter saw Granny Colston. She was bending over her rockery, gardening. Under her carefully tended flowers was her own shelter where she could hide from the bomb. The bomb!

Peter opened his eyes with a bump. He found himself staring at the walls of his cave. Pale green tufts of grass grew out of the cracks and crevices of the rock. Little beetles and spiders scuttled busily, going about their daily lives.

Vikram was right. What was the use of hiding from the bomb? What was the use of being safe inside if everyone he loved was outside?

Feeling calmer, Peter roused himself and scavenged among the toppled tins for something to eat. Chaser wagged his tail expectantly. He must be hungry, too. He opened a tin of baked beans and tipped them into a bowl. The dog devoured them in two gulps and panted for more. Peter opened another tin for him, feeling a little guilty. Baked beans were all Jack would eat and now there was only one tin left.

Peter opened a tin of macaroni cheese for himself and consumed it almost as quickly as Chaser. The stock of macaroni was getting low too. If he stayed here much longer he would be forced to eat artichoke hearts and asparagus tips.

Energy restored, Chaser dashed out of the cave. Peter wriggled out after him. They rushed in and out of the stream splashing and gulping the cool water. Then Peter tossed sticks for Chaser. No matter how many sticks he tossed, Chaser chased after even the twentieth stick with as much enthusiasm as the first.

He heard a distant owl call and stood stock-still. Chaser too froze, his ears cocked, his tail taut. They heard it again, and another, overlapping the first. It must be Jack and Charlotte. They were back.

With a surge of joy Peter leapt up the rock face to where the long grass grew. He plucked a blade of grass and blew through it. It screeched and made an ugly sound, but they heard it and answered. Unable to contain himself he ran from the clearing, springing down the

hillside like a mountain goat, with Chaser barking and
bounding at his side.

Peter couldn't know how wild he had become. There
were no mirrors in the hideaway. His hair hung long and
tangled with thorns and leaves. His skin was darker,
scratched and blotched with mud and water. When he
plunged through the thicket, all bare arms and legs, and
leapt on to the track before Jack and Charlotte he couldn't
know how savage he looked. Even his eyes were like those
of a wild animal, darting around on the lookout for danger,
his muscles taut, ready to flee.

They stared at him in shocked silence. Then Jack
whispered, 'Have you become a hippy, Peter?'

Peter didn't answer. He didn't understand, but looked at them blankly. 'The hippies have gone,' he said finally. His voice shook a little. 'The Corries drove them away.'

Chaser came trotting up with a stick clenched tightly between his jaws. Peter tussled with him to free it, then hurled it as far as he could throw down the hillside. Chaser disappeared in a flurry of paws and fur and twigs.

'That's their dog, isn't it?' Charlotte spoke for the first time.

'Yeah!' said Peter proudly. 'That's Chaser. He got left behind somehow, so now he's living with me.'

'Aren't you ever going home?' asked Jack looking bewildered.

'I dunno,' frowned Peter. 'I don't know what'll happen to me if I go home. Anyway, I'd never be allowed to keep Chaser. I'll wait till they come and get him.'

'What if they don't come back?' asked Charlotte.

Peter shrugged. 'I dunno.'

The three children began walking on up towards the hideaway. As they got nearer Jack got more excited, and began running on ahead. 'What was it like sleeping in the cave?' he shouted. 'Were you scared? Were there wild animals and things? Did you really stay here all the time alone?'

Peter looked at Charlotte. Her face was sober. She gave him a small smile and held out a carrier bag. 'I've brought some tea for you,' she said quietly.

They arrived at the cave. Jack had already rushed in and out three times before they got there. Charlotte didn't comment when she saw the mess the cave was in.

There were empty tins and half-empty tins all jumbled up with the full tins and empty packets of crisps.

'There's not much left,' said Peter ruefully. 'Me and Chaser ate most of the beans. I'll get some more. I've still got my five pounds.'

'That store was supposed to last us all three weeks if they dropped the bomb,' cried Charlotte.

'I've been thinking,' said Peter. 'About the bomb . . .'

'So have we,' interrupted Jack pushing in between them.

'We don't want to go into the cave if they drop the bomb,' explained Charlotte. 'Not if it means leaving behind all the people we love – and there really isn't room for everyone, is there?'

'I was thinking the same,' muttered Peter. Who were the people he loved? Andy, Granny Colston, Mum? And the hippies? Vikram? They would all be left ouside if the bomb dropped. 'Let's just keep it as our den,' he said.

Charlotte cleared the table and unpacked the contents of her carrier bag. There were several marmite sandwiches, three sausage rolls and half a dozen fairy cakes.

Peter took a marmite sandwich, then couldn't resist stuffing another into his mouth before he was halfway through the first, and before he had finished the second marmite sandwich, he stuffed a fairy cake into his mouth on top of that.

'Ugh!' exclaimed Jack, who couldn't take his eyes of Peter. 'How can you eat marmite and fairy cakes together?'

Peter's mouth was too full to answer.

The dog began barking furiously outside the cave. Peter crouched at the spy-hole and peered through to the clearing. Jack and Charlotte heard him draw in his breath sharply.

'What is it?' whispered Charlotte. 'Have the police come?'

'Or the Corries?' asked Jack looking frightened.

'It's Vikram!' breathed Peter. 'I knew he'd come back.' Peter slid out of the cave almost shyly. There was no point in wondering how Vikram knew he was here.

They stood facing each other. There was no need for speech. Their thoughts flew silently between them.

'You must go home now,' Vikram's face told him.

'Must I?' Peter's eyes pleaded. 'Must I go back to school uniform and school, to homework and violin practice, to silent tea times with Annabel? Why can't I live with you. You can teach me?'

Vikram read his thoughts. He crossed the stream and came up to Peter. He pressed his thumb to the middle of his forehead, and spoke softly. 'Do you know,' he said, 'just here you have a third eye. It is the eye of the soul and sees far more than the two eyes outside your head, that is, if you learn to use it. This is the eye of knowledge. Not the knowledge that teachers teach you, but the knowledge of knowing. Whatever happens on the outside, if you are strong inside, then nothing matters.'

They stood at the stream watching the water hurling itself over the edge of the waterfall. 'You know,' said Vikram, 'They do say life is just a bubble.'

Jack and Charlotte came out, mystified by the silence. They stood on either side of Peter protectively.

'It's all right now,' Vikram told them. 'Peter is going home.'

Charlotte's face broke into a wide smile. Without a word, she went back into the cave and methodically collected together Peter's belongings.

'I'll let you ride my bike whenever you want,' whispered Jack.

Peter nodded.

Vikram slipped the rope lead over Chaser's head and then they all walked down through the woods and on to the road. Charlotte and Jack found their bikes and they continued walking together to the edge of the water meadows. Vikram stood within the boundary of the trees.

'I'll say goodbye here,' he said. 'I'll always know how you are, and we'll meet again one summer.' Once more he pressed his thumb against Peter's forehead. 'Remember,' his eyes told him silently.

Peter, Jack and Charlotte stepped out of the shade of Juggins Wood and into the calm, early evening light which hung over the water meadows and glistened in the streams and brooks. Peter knew he had stepped back into the eye of his mirror, back into his room. Already he had gone home. They walked past the brown and white cows, who looked as if they had been grazing there since the world began, and on into the village.

When they reached Peter's gate, he said 'I'll be all right now.' Then he walked up the path to Trimble Cottage.

The bike was leaning up against the shed. It was bright and shiny. It was brand-new. There was a note tied to the handlebars: 'Welcome home, Peter. I love you. Mum.'

Peter turned round to Jack and Charlotte, still standing at the gate. 'I'll see you tomorrow,' he said, then he opened the kitchen door and went inside.